SURFACE TENSION

COLONY FIVE MARS

GERALD M KILBY

OUTER PLANET
MEDIA

For notifications on upcoming books, and access to my FREE starter library, please join my Readers Group at www.geraldmkilby.com.

CONTENTS

1

DUST STORM

Things started breaking down. Small things at first, mostly inconsequential glitches—minor problems that always occur in highly technical environments, such as the one that had developed over the preceding decades on Mars. But as the dust storm grew in both intensity and duration, the number of these minor occurrences started to rise exponentially.

Yet dust storms were a fact of life on Mars. So, the citizens did what they always did: batten down the hatches and ride it out. It helped that the technology, which had been developed to provide life support in this harsh, deadly environment, had also evolved to cope with all that the weather on the planet could throw at it.

Well, almost all.

Every system was affected. Air intakes clogged, causing vital machinery to overheat and eventually fail. Fine dust clung to every surface, rendering solar panels effectively useless. The dust penetrated deep into every gap and crack, abrading seals and bearings to the point of destruction. The fine grains even entered into the habitats, and no amount of filtration and decontamination could keep it out. And with it came the fear of exposure to increased levels of perchlorate, which was highly toxic to humans. Soon, the infirmaries noticed an uptick in admissions.

Increased ionization in the outside atmosphere played havoc with communications systems, rendering data transmission problematic. The fledgling Martian GPS system struggled to cope with drop-outs and maintaining accuracy. Voice communications fared better, but only because of the human brain's ability to make sense of even the most garbled message. That, and the fall back to using analog transmission when digital systems finally failed.

Yet by sol seventy-five, as the dust storm grew to encompass the entire planet, radiation levels on the surface had reached a new high watermark. They had been steadily increasing since the beginning of the storm. However, radiation posed no real threat to human health; shielding technology was such that they were well protected from its ill effects. But delicate electronics did not fare so well, particularly those more exposed to the surface environment. The most susceptible components to malfunction and failure were microprocessors, those ubiquitous little black squares that populate almost every technological unit in existence. No control system had been designed that did not have circuitry running code through a microprocessor of some kind. They were the small army of silicon workers that kept civilization functioning.

Yet those designed for space applications in general, and Martian operation in particular, were hardened against high radiation levels. They had redundancy built in, with a doubling and sometimes tripling of circuitry, allowing operations to run in parallel and be cross-checked for errors. But all this additional processing required more power, more power created more heat, more heat required more cooling, and with the majority of cooling systems on Mars utilizing the ambient temperature of the atmosphere—a sufficiently chilly minus 60 degrees Celsius—this method was severely compromised by the incessant dust bunging up the works. As the increased radiation bombarded these silicon substrates, the error rate increased, consuming more power and increasing the heat generation until the unit ultimately failed. The strange thing was, no one saw it coming.

By sol one hundred and twenty-two, they had finally run out of spare parts for pretty much everything. All surplus energy was now diverted into the manufacture of components just to keep up with the failure rate. But where most mechanical components and some electrical components could be manufactured on Mars in the primary industrial city of Syrtis, no such facility existed for the fabrication of microprocessors. The citizens of Mars relied solely on importing them from Earth.

But when the dust storm entered its two hundred and fourteenth sol, the rate of systems failure finally outpaced the rate at which they could be repaired. From that point on, entropy gained the upper hand, and they were now fighting a losing battle.

And so, by sol two hundred and forty of the planet-wide dust storm, it was clear to the government on Mars that the situation was becoming critical, and that emergency powers were needed to take control of the resources. It was a move they had been reluctant to invoke for fear of spooking the already nervous citizens. But the rate of accident and death due to systems failure had already reached unprecedented levels, and people were understandably rattled. Something radical needed to be done. Yet the decision wasn't made until a CO_2 scrubber failed in an isolated waystation just north of Elysium, killing fourteen people in their sleep.

All nonessential operations were to cease with immediate effect. All mining and processing that did not contribute directly to the manufacture of spare parts was shut down. All scientific research ceased, and all research stations closed. All citizens were ordered to evacuate outlying outposts and waystations and return immediately to one of the two main population centers in either Jezero or Syrtis. All traffic on the surface was forbidden unless absolutely essential, and all visitors and tourists were to leave immediately.

And so began a great exodus of people off the planet, back to Earth or to one of the many hotels orbiting the planet, where they could wait out the dust storm in relative comfort.

Soon, most activity on Mars began to literally grind to a halt. Jezero, the seat of government but primarily a tourist destination, was hollowed out. Those that worked to service this industry were left idle. Bars and cafes were shuttered, parks and nonessential sectors were shut down, and large swaths of the population were relocated to conserve energy and resources. Similar reorganization of the civil and industrial society was also happening in Syrtis.

Of course, the pervading assumption was that the dust storm had to end eventually, and that everything would then get back to normal. Yet the devil makes work for idle minds, and soon the main population centers were awash with rumor and counter-rumor, and a sense of foreboding started to take root. Some said that the situation was far worse than officials were claiming, and that they were all doomed—it was only a matter of time. Others suggested that human activity on Mars, coupled with a number of terraforming experiments, had caused a major increase in the surface temperature—the source of energy that was driving the dust storm—and by consequence it could potentially last for years, maybe even decades.

There were even some in Jezero who suggested that there was no real shortage of spare parts. That it was in fact Syrtis that was stockpiling and preventing Jezero from accessing vital supplies, just so they could undermine the seat of government. Meanwhile, some in Syrtis postulated that Jezero only invoked martial law so they could take control of the fledgling administration running their city. Some even suggested that the government had already evacuated with the tourists, relocating up to the orbitals and effectively leaving the citizens of Mars to fend for themselves.

And so it was that, by sol two hundred and seventy, society on Mars finally started to break down.

2

BREAKDOWN

In the center of the situation room of the Martian Law and Order Department (MLOD), Major Mia Sorelli stood and studied a large, imposing screen that took up most of one wall. Its function was to give a graphical synopsis of the current incidents and their status all across Jezero City. It was a sea of blinking red and orange, like some festive display of all that was wrong in the metropolis. She shook her head and sighed.

Even with the current population in Jezero down to just ninety-five thousand after the tourists had abandoned the place, Mia and her team were still stretched to the very limits of their abilities. Never before had she witnessed such an escalation of social mayhem, not even back in New York during the blackout, and that was saying something. But these were not crimes of profit or opportunity, or some gangland feud. No, these were the crimes of the desperate, the traumatized, and the angry.

Mia despaired for the human race. Here they all were, being slowly etched out of existence one grain of sand at a time, heading for collapse, and all the people wanted to do was protest, occupy, riot, and cause as much mayhem as possible—as if this would somehow save them. It was madness, and it wasn't much better over in Syrtis. Now was the time for society to pull together and work for the greater good, for their very survival. Instead, fear and paranoia had taken over, as if some unseen malaise had infected the population. It was every man, woman, and child for themselves. At least, that was how Mia Sorelli saw it.

"Things seem to be calming down a bit today."

Mia turned her head to see Lieutenant Bret Stanton standing beside her, also studying the screen. "I admire your optimism, Bret. Ever consider you might just be delusional?"

"No, seriously. Today is the first time in two weeks that we've had a decrease in new incidents. And guess what else I heard?"

Mia looked back at the screen. "Don't tell me, we're all going to die?"

Bret gave an exasperated sigh. "The density of dust particles has dropped again this sol. That's two sols in a row. That's good news. It could mean the dust storm is finally running out of energy."

"They say that all the time, Bret. But only when it goes down, which happens less than going up. Don't get your hopes up—it still means we're all going to die."

"Why are you so pessimistic all the time, Mia? Don't you want this to end?"

"I'm not pessimistic, I'm just not delusional like you."

"Suit yourself. But I for one have some faith in our ability to get through this." Bret's eyes locked onto the screen again, and he went rigid. "Oh crap."

"What now?" Mia scanned the display. A bright red marker flashed over a food production facility in the northwestern sector of Jezero City, about a kilometer away.

"It's a Code 43." Bret pointed at a sidebar on the screen that had begun to display data on the incident. It was a technical failure, the worst kind: loss of atmosphere. "We'd better send some people over there."

"We don't have any spare resources," said Mia. "Just leave it. It's a systems failure—let the techs deal with it for now. We do nothing unless they ask." Mia could see that Bret was just itching to help, but he stayed silent. He might have been a little naive, but not so much that he didn't know the score. There was only so much the MLOD could do with the limited resources they had available.

They both stood in silence for a while and watched the display. The incident began to escalate. First, a call flashed up for medical assistance. That meant people were injured, or worse, dead. Then it came, the call neither of them wanted to see: crowd control.

"Shit," said Mia. "It must be bad."

"I'll go," said Bret.

Mia sighed and looked around at the three other people in the room—all techs, all needed to manage and coordinate the ongoing operations of the MLOD. Mia shouted out to them, "I need two armed guards. Find them for me, take them from anywhere you can, I don't care. Send them to the Code 43, and we'll meet them on the way." She turned to Bret. "Come on, we'll do it together. I have a feeling this one could get ugly."

They hurried out of the operations room and headed for the incident at Agri-dome B428.

THEY WERE ABOUT HALFWAY there when a small, autonomous ground car rolled up beside them with two guards that had got the call from central to divert to the incident. Mia and Bret hopped in, and the car sped off.

"So, what are we dealing with here, Major?" one of the guards asked Mia as he checked his plasma pistol.

"We've got a blowout in a small agri-dome in sector B428. It's undergoing critical decompression. The good news, if you could call it that, is the safety systems kicked in and sealed the doors, so the rupture is contained. The bad news is there are people still inside, slowly running out of breathable air."

The guard shook his head. "How long have they got?"

"Techs are saying ten to fifteen minutes," said Bret.

"Poor bastards. What a way to go."

They brought the car to a halt a few meters from the back of a large crowd of around fifty people that had gathered at the main entrance to the agri-dome. The group parted as a tech with a bloodied forehead pushed his way through and out to where Mia and her crew had just disembarked from the ground car. "You gotta stop them... They're trying to open the door... You gotta stop them... If they cut open that door, then we're all dead."

"What happened?" said Mia.

"They jumped us... Couldn't stop them... Took our plasma cutter. You gotta stop it."

Already, the two guards were beating a path through the assembled onlookers. Mia, Bret, and the injured tech followed in their wake.

"Stand aside. Out of the way." They pushed back the crowd, weapons ready just in case anybody had a mind to argue with them. As they came closer to the main door of the small agri-dome, Mia could see the reflected light of the plasma cutter strobing off the wall and ceiling, illuminating the drama that was unfolding. One man worked the cutter as five others stood guard around him, facing the crowd, all holding crude weapons. They were trying to prevent anyone from stopping them getting the door to the decompressing agri-dome open.

"They're going to kill us all. This is crazy." Shouts emanated from the crowd as Mia and her team converged on the area in front of the door.

"Okay, that's enough. I want you to put down the weapons and step away from the door."

"No goddamn way, there's people still inside... My brother is in there... We're not leaving them to die." He stood his ground, gripping a stout metal bar tighter in his hands.

"I'm not asking again." Mia unholstered her plasma pistol and dialed it up a notch from stun. He was a big guy, so she wanted to make sure she could take him down with just one shot. She aimed it at him. "Do it now."

Nobody moved; the guy operating the plasma cutter continued working. Through the small window in the door, Mia could see the fear etched into the faces on the other side. She fired.

A blue ball of crackling fury hit the nearest of the group protecting the guys working on the door. It sent him flying back, bouncing off the dome wall. More shots were fired, people screamed and ran, and the plasma cutter stopped. The air smelled of ozone and burnt flesh.

One of the guards grabbed the limp body near the door and dragged it away, as if for some unknown reason it might suddenly reanimate and continue trying to open the door. The others now turned to face the crowd, weapons at the ready.

"Everyone needs to evacuate this area...*now!*" Mia shouted as forcefully as she could.

There was a momentary silence. All that could be heard was the frantic banging on the door from inside the doomed agri-dome, as those still alive inside realized that all hope of their salvation was now lost.

"You bastards... There's people still alive in there, and they're going to die because you." Someone dashed forward, a young woman. "My father is in there," she screamed.

But she had barely enough time to utter the word before she was cut down by a shot from Mia's pistol. She took the blast square in the chest and collapsed on the floor, a mesh of electrical craziness fizzling and crackling all over her as it slowly dissipated.

"I said everybody outta here, now!" Mia shouted.

The crowd started to thin out, mumbling obscenities as they went. It took a few minutes for them to disperse, during which time the banging from inside the door ceased. The medics arrived, followed by another team of techs and several more guards. A cordon was erected, and finally Mia felt it safe enough to put her weapon away. She let out a long, deep breath and felt the adrenaline drain from her body. She shook.

"You okay?" Bret's hand rested on her shoulder.

Mia took a moment. "Yeah...sort of." She looked around at the carnage and slowly shook her head again. "When will this ever end?"

Bret gave a slow nod. "It's okay, the situation has de-escalated now."

Mia shot him a glance. "It's far from okay, Bret. Look at this." She swept a hand around the area littered with the fallen.

"They'll be okay... They're just stunned, banged up a bit. They'll live."

Mia remained silent, her gaze resting on the young

woman she'd just shot. "We're coming apart at the seams, Bret. How long can this go on?"

"They didn't get the door open, Mia. Imagine the chaos if they did."

"Maybe not this time. But people are getting more desperate. How long before something really catastrophic happens? And it will happen. It's only a matter of time."

But before Bret could answer, Mia's earpiece bleeped. She tapped the side of her ear. "Yeah, what is it?"

The voice of an operator in the situation room echoed in Mia's ear. "Incident at sector C27. Looting in progress—backup required."

"Okay, we're on our way." She tapped the earpiece off and turned to Bret. "The day ain't over yet. Trouble at C27. Call the others. Leave one guard here, and let's get to where we're needed next."

"Sure." Bret moved off to relay the instructions.

Mia took a moment to gather her wits. She took a deep breath and tried to calm the dread that seemed to seep up from her very core. "Easy girl," she said to herself. "It's just another day at the office."

3

POE TARKIN

W hen Mia got a call that Poe Tarkin, Director General of Martian Security, wanted to meet her in his chambers, she assumed the worst. Her handling of the incident the previous sol at the agri-dome was not one of Mia's finest hours. It might have been acceptable except for the fact that she had not checked her plasma pistol when she had shot the young woman. If she had, she would have realized that it hadn't been set back to stun. Instead, it was one notch up. Now, the young woman was hospitalized, and would take quite some time to recover. That being said, it could have been worse. Mia could have killed her.

In Mia's mind, this was just one more error of judgment in a long line that she had accumulated since she had been given the job as head of the new MLOD in Jezero City. That was six years ago. Back then, she had no idea how much the population on Mars would explode.

Now, there were over half a million in two main cities. Fortunately, she only had Jezero to deal with, but even that had ballooned in size and complexity over the intervening years.

Yet despite the ever-increasing responsibility and pressure, she could have handled it if it wasn't for the dust storm—367 sols and counting, the longest and most intense storm ever recorded on Mars. It would never end, and even if it did, Mia doubted she would live to see it.

Tarkin's chambers were located in the administrative sector, the oldest area of Jezero City, which had its roots in the colony's foundation. The building itself was relatively new, one of a great many that had sprouted up in the last number of years. It was a five-story oblong structure, which was the new architectural style—a move away from the domed buildings of the past. Mia was met at the entrance lobby by an aide who politely shepherded her through a series of rigorous security checks and then along winding corridors up to the top floor, finally depositing her outside a set of imposing, highly polished faux-wooden doors with an aura of antiquity and ostentatiousness in equal measure. The aide opened one door and signaled with the sweep of an arm for her to enter.

Mia had met Poe many times, but had not had a reason recently to visit him in his new chambers, so this was her first time entering the room. Judging by the imposing door, she had imagined it to be some grand hall fit for a king, so she was surprised to find it much smaller than in her imagination. It was around seven meters long and half that wide. One wall was all windows looking out across Jezero City, except there was nothing to see—just a thick brown fog. Here and there she could make out the ghostly glow of navigation beacons on the tops of buildings and communication towers, but none of the actual structures could be made out.

Opposite this wall, Poe Tarkin sat behind a large, functional desk. He rose to greet her, a hand extended. "Mia, good to see you. Glad you could make it." They shook hands, and he gestured at a seat in front of the desk. "Sit." Then he turned to an ornate sideboard and reached in. "Drink?"

Mia took a moment to get her bearings. She was expecting a dressing down, maybe even a demotion, but this meeting seemed to be something different. "Eh, sure."

"Bourbon? I believe that's your preferred poison?"

"Bourbon sounds good."

She took the glass Poe presented to her. They clinked. "To health, wealth, and happiness, in your preferred order," said Poe.

Mia took a sip. It was smooth and ambrosial, and she suspected it was the real deal all the way from source, not some Martian knock-off. A fantastically expensive luxury, and she was surprised at Poe offering it to her. Perhaps this meeting was something else entirely; far from her being balled out, it seemed that he wanted something from her, something she may not want to give—hence the drink, a way of buttering her up.

He took his seat behind the desk and leaned back. "I

heard you had a bit of trouble over at one of the agri-domes."

Mia sighed and wondered if she had read it all wrong, clung to hope where none existed. "Yeah, things...eh, got a little out of hand."

Poe leaned in with an avuncular look. "These are trying times, Mia. People are on edge. I didn't bring you here to pass judgment on your actions, in case that's what you're thinking. You did what you had to do...what one always has to do in far from ideal circumstances." He paused for a beat. "You'll be happy to hear that the young woman will make a full recovery. So, don't beat yourself up over it."

Mia nodded. "Thanks for letting me know, but..."

"But what? It's over. Forget it."

Mia looked into her drink like she was trying to extract some deeper meaning from the arrangement of ice cubes. "It's all going to rat shit." She looked up at Poe. "Everything is breaking down. The people are scared and frightened and loosing hope. How do you keep a lid on that?"

Poe leaned back, and it was his turn to sigh. "I'll not insult your intelligence, Mia, by trying to sugarcoat the seriousness of the predicament we are in, or the precariousness of our situation. But hold the line we must. The people need to be assured that we can make it through this." He leaned in again and pointed a finger at Mia. "And we *can* get through it. You need to believe this."

"It's hard to believe when all I see is the slow, steady

breakdown of society. How all sense of human decency gets jettisoned as soon as the shit hits the fan. I'll be honest, Poe...sometimes I truly despair for humanity."

"Yes, well we've all been tested during these times. I too feel it, but I try not to let those thoughts cloud my judgment."

"Then you're made of stronger stuff than me. What's it been...nearly 370 sols—over one Earth year—since this dust storm started."

She cocked an eyebrow at Poe. "Some say it's our fault. All this human activity on Mars has raised the temperature of the surface, creating more energy for the storm. Some believe it will never end."

"Scientists." Poe waved a dismissive hand. "They say a lot of things. Who knows for sure? All we can do is deal with what's in front of us, find a way to get through this, or find a way to live with it."

He went silent for a moment, his attention drawn to some object on his desk. He picked up a small, flat black square and held it between his thumb and forefinger. "It's hard to believe that this...innocuous looking object, would prove to be our Achilles heel."

"Microchips?"

"Microprocessors, to be precise. Those ubiquitous little black squares that populate every single technological unit on this planet, not to mention Earth. So ubiquitous, in fact, that we take them for granted. This"—he held it up for Mia to see—"is truly the culmination of humanity's technological power. Honed to perfection and hardened to withstand all that Mars can throw at it... That is, until now. It seems nothing we currently have can withstand the toxic cocktail of electrical mayhem and cosmic radiation that now exists on the planet's surface."

"What about the emergency shipments from Earth?"

Poe set the chip on the desk and leaned back. "It has taken longer than expected to design chips that can withstand the new environmental realities, and get them tested and manufactured. Then, of course, there is the long journey from Earth. As it stands, we're only getting a quarter of what was promised. The shipments that have arrived are far less than we need."

Mia finished the last of her drink. "So, Poe, why am I here? I can't imagine you brought me here just to discuss the limitations of current chip fabrication?"

Poe gave a smile. "No, you're right. I didn't." He paused for a beat, as if choosing his next words carefully. "I have a job that needs doing, one that I think best suits your particular talents."

"Oh?" Mia gave him a circumspect look. "And what particular talents would those be?"

"Let me explain the situation first. A few hours ago, word came to us that Dan Frazer, an MLOD agent in Syrtis, was found dead in his quarters."

"Frazer is dead?" Mia was genuinely shocked.

"I'm afraid so. Sad news. I believe you knew him well —he was a native of Jezero City."

"I did know him. He was a good guy. How did it happen?"

"Apparently the CO_2 scrubber in the accommodation module failed, and he died in his sleep. They only found him a few hours ago, when he didn't show up for work."

Mia shook her head. "That's just...terrible."

There was a moment's silence as they both contemplated the tragedy.

"I need you to go to Syrtis and bring the body back here to Jezero. He was one of us and an important member of the team, so we need someone from within the department to do this. There will be some diplomatic duties surrounding the handover; that's why it needs to be someone senior who performs this duty."

Mia sighed. "Sounds like a convenient reason to get me out of the way for a while."

Poe raised a hand. "Don't start thinking like that, Mia. Granted, we in the department feel that you're heading for burnout as you try to keep a lid on things. But who isn't these sols? We're all feeling the pressure. That being said, this needs to be done and... Well, your name came up, and we feel you're the best person for the job."

"The job of being an undertaker."

"There's more to it." He lowered his voice. "We don't think it was an accident."

Mia sat up. "You're saying he was murdered?"

"I'm saying it's a possibility, and that's where you come in. Let's face it, with your background and training as an investigator, you're the best we have. Your talents are wasted trying to be a SWAT team leader. The department here can survive without you for a while."

Mia shifted in her seat. She had to admit that taking some time away from trying to quell social unrest on a daily basis sounded good to her. But, as always, there were some downsides. Syrtis was not Jezero; she would be entering unknown territory, she wouldn't know her way around, where to begin, or who to trust. It could be perilous.

For one, it was a much bigger city, an industrial heartland. Where Jezero had undergone a quasi-gentrification process by virtue of being the seat of government and the main tourist town, Syrtis had rapidly developed as the primary industrial engine on Mars. It was four times the population of Jezero, most of whom were permanent citizens, unlike here, where at least half were tourists—and those had all gone now. What's more, Syrtis's rapid expansion had seen it fracture into several competing factions, mainly led by corporations, none of whom were predisposed to the Martian government in Jezero. Mia was under no illusion as to the hornets' nest of vested interests and political backstabbing that went on in Syrtis. It was like the Wild West, where a badge only meant something so long as you were prepared to back it up with firepower.

"Syrtis is a snake pit. Sounds to me like you're taking me out of the frying pan and dumping me in the fire."

Poe leaned in, placed his elbows on the desk, and opened his hands. "Look, Mia, Frazer was an agent of this department, and therefore a representative of the government of Mars, so we can't just let this go. We can't appear to ignore the possibility that someone, or some group, had him killed. And I understand that our authority over Syrtis is tenuous at best, but we need to at least be seen doing something."

"So, what backup will I have?"

"The MLOD in Syrtis will assist you. But I'll be honest, they're all a bit spooked, and their reach is—how can I put it?—less that we would like it to be."

"In other words, they're worse than useless. Great."

"Frazer was our best man there, and his loss will be felt deeply within the department. If nothing else, your visit will help shore up morale."

"So, this is really a public relations job."

"Partly." Poe glanced down at a personal display on his desk and tapped a few times. "Chief Becker, who is now the current department head over there, will meet you at the freight terminal when the caravan arrives in two days."

Mia sat up. "Caravan? You mean I won't be taking a shuttle?"

Poe shook his head. "There are very few shuttle flights at the moment. In fact, there are virtually none, except for extreme emergencies. So, you'll be taking the overland freight caravan. Believe me, it's safer."

"But Syrtis is like fifteen hundred kilometers away."

"Twelve, to be exact. But it travels nonstop, so you'll be there in twenty-four hours. It's the only safe way to get there now. It's like a train with multiple connected units, so there's plenty of redundancy built in. If one of the units breaks down, it doesn't affect the rest—it just keeps right on going."

Mia gave him a look as if to say, *Yeah, right*. She stood and walked over to the long window and tried to see out. There was nothing but the vague outline of buildings wrapped in a dense brown fog. Few people went out in it unless there was no other option, so spending a full twenty-four hours traveling across the surface of Mars was still a risky proposition. Yet as Mia peered into the dust, she felt it pull on her like a perilous escape route might tempt a prisoner. It was a way out, of sorts.

She would do it. She would take the mission.

Mia turned around to face Poe, who was still seated behind his desk. "I'm going to need a droid, and not some dumb service machine. I need one of the diagnostic and analysis droids."

Poe shook his head apologetically. "We simply don't have any, Mia. They are all offline or being used as spare parts for the service droids." He opened his hands. "There's none available."

"Then what you're asking me to do is impossible. If I'm to go snooping around where my badge is meaning-less, then I'll need a droid that can do some hacking and system bypassing. I can't do that myself."

"I'm sorry, Mia. I understand, and if there was any way I could get you one, I would. But there just isn't."

Mia thought for a moment. She reached up and scratched her chin before slowly pointing a finger at Poe. "There is one. Gizmo."

Poe stood with an incredulous look. "Gizmo? You can't be serious. It was decommissioned years ago. It's just a relic, like all the other G2 units."

"It's nothing like an old G2 unit. In fact, it's in many ways far superior to any of these newer droids we've got."

"Yeah, but there was a good reason it was decommissioned. You know all the political trouble that droid caused... It's a hot potato."

"Well, exceptional times require exceptional measures. I can't do anything without a diagnostic droid."

Poe was shaking his head in disbelief, or maybe it was at the realization that Mia was right. "I don't know... I mean, does it even still exist? I'm afraid I've lost track of where it ended up."

"It still exists, and it's still intact, as far as I know."

"Where?"

"It's an exhibit in the museum."

Poe considered Mia for a moment before sitting down again.

Mia used this as an opportunity to push her case. "I can't do what you want without a droid."

Poe sighed. "Okay, we can try to reactivate it." He shook his head again. "There's going to be hell to pay when the council finds out."

Mia smiled. "Well that's your problem, Poe."

4

MUSEUM

There were two fundamental problems in attempting to reactivate the old droid. The first, and the one that concerned Poe Tarkin the most, was political. Gizmo had been decommissioned under an extraordinary mandate issued by the ruling council of Mars. At the time, its almost sentient nature had been viewed by some as a security threat, and the fact it had been deemed to have gone rogue. Not that the little robot was entirely to blame for this action, as it was simply responding to the instructions of some very influential people in Martian governmental hierarchy—Dr. Jann Malbec, to name one.

But Mia had also played a significant role in its ultimate fall from grace. They had been in a few scrapes together where people had been killed, albeit in self-defense. Nevertheless, Gizmo had an array of lethal weaponry at its disposal and wasn't afraid to use any of it.

So, it was simply deemed too dangerous to wander around an ever-expanding colony.

Yet the little droid had history; it went way back almost to the very foundation of the colony, and as such, it was also seen as a sort of national treasure. If it were to be decommissioned, then it should at least be given the recognition it deserved and treated with a modicum of respect. It was decided in the end that it would be powered down and placed on permanent exhibition in the new museum that was being established. It was not to be dismantled, save for the removal of all weaponry, and not to be reactivated again under any circumstances.

So what Mia was proposing, by rights, should require council approval, something that would be very difficult to obtain at this late hour. But Poe, to his credit, was not overly concerned with this. He conceded to Mia's argument that things had moved on. The colony was now full of semi-sentient droids, some far more sophisticated than Gizmo ever was, at least until the dust storm hit. So, in that sense, Gizmo was no longer a threat, and the current council could easily be persuaded of that.

In the end, the director of planetary security agreed to Mia's demands, and so the second problem became the real issue—was it even technically possible to reanimate the droid after all this time? Mia's answer to this was, "Well, there's only one way to find out."

. . .

AN HOUR or so after her meeting with Poe Tarkin, Mia found herself standing in front of the main entrance door to the Jezero City Foundation Museum with a two-person tech team who were busying themselves trying to get the door open. The museum, like most of the other infrastructure utilized by the city's burgeoning tourist industry, had been mothballed—put into a low-energy maintenance mode. Some sectors had been shut down completely, but the delicate nature of some of the exhibits in the museum required it to have a minimum of life support.

"Got it," shouted Max, one of the techs. The double doors of the museum entrance gently swung open.

It was pitch black inside. Maintenance mode, it seemed, did not stretch to include illumination, so they moved by flashlight. Max and the other tech, Jackie, each pushed a trolley laden with tools and test equipment. Mia considered all this equipment a bad sign, not that she had thought reanimating Gizmo would be as simple as pressing the *on* button. But both Max and Jackie had been very keen to impress on her just how technically challenging this enterprise was, although Mia got the feeling that they were both up to the challenge. She supposed that bringing some ancient technology back to life was something different from their normal routine of doing whatever it took to keep some ailing systems from dying.

Mia had only visited the museum once, a long time ago now, and that was just to see Gizmo's final resting place, so her memory of the layout was vague. She knew it was housed in one of the older domes in the colony, a former bio-dome probably some fifty meters in diameter. But it was impossible to see more than what their feeble flashlights could illuminate.

Jackie took the lead, flashlight strapped to her head. She had a slate clipped to the handle of the trolley and was reading their location on a map displayed on the screen. "This way." She pointed straight ahead and took off at a slow, cautious pace. The others followed.

As they walked, Mia began to pick out vague shapes of ancient spacecraft looming out of the gloom. She swung her light over some of these to get a sense of what they might be. She stopped in front of the squat, battered shape of an early lander. It was around ten meters wide and less than that tall. Its surface bore all the marks of a violent journey through the Martian atmosphere, its heat shield scorched and blackened. She stood and looked at it for a moment, wondering what sort of crazy lunatic would even consider going to Mars in such a tiny vessel. But those were the early days, a long time ago now.

Beside it, her light picked up the form of even older technology. A small, six-wheel robotic rover. She moved her light to read the text on the plaque in front of the display. It told her she was looking at the Mars 2020 rover, the very first human mission to land in Jezero Crater. She swept her light over it again now that she had some idea what she was looking at. There was no doubting it was primitive, but still impressive given it was the vanguard of humanity's eventual colonization of Mars.

"Found it," Max shouted. Mia looked around to see the tech waving at her while Jackie started unpacking equipment. When Mia caught up with them, they had set up some floor lights to provide better illumination to work with.

This section of the museum housed an exhibition of robots and service droids that had been utilized during the early years of the colony. The early versions tended to be wheeled or use tracks, like Gizmo, whereas the later versions became quadrupeds, and some bipeds, the latter almost humanlike in size and form. Gizmo took up the central position in this long evolutionary line of robotic workers, more by virtue of its physical appearance: tracked wheels, as well as a somewhat ungainly and unsophisticated look. But what Gizmo lacked in physical sophistication it more than made up for in the high functioning of its general intelligence. None of the other droids in this exhibit even came close to Gizmo's level of analytical thinking. Ultimately, that was what proved its undoing; it was just too smart for its own good.

Max set up and adjusted some floor lights as Jackie removed the rope that cordoned the visitors off from the exhibits. She stepped up onto the plinth where Gizmo sat and gave it a visual inspection. "An old G2 unit. You don't see many of these anymore, even now, when we're trying to press everything into service because of the storm." She turned back to Mia. "Are you sure this is the one you're looking for? It's pretty much an antique." She waved her hand, pointing farther up the line of droid exhibits. "Maybe we could get some of these others working for you. Any of those would be better than this bucket of servos."

Mia had to admit that in the gloom of a mothballed museum, the little robot looked almost forlorn. Its casing was scratched and battered, and its head hung down over its breastplate. It looked a far different machine than the one she remembered all those years ago, in happier times. For a brief moment she considered that maybe this was all a bad idea. In fact, the entire mission that Poe Tarkin was proposing was a bad idea. She could just refuse to go. Poe couldn't force her; he would just get someone else. But that would mean that she would be back on the frontline tomorrow, with the thankless task of holding the line against the ever-increasing social unrest and the incessant unraveling of colony society. If nothing else, this mission would give her a break from dealing with the demands of leading a team that faced an impossible task.

"This is the one." She pointed at Gizmo. "How long do you think it will take to reactivate it?"

Both techs were now circling the machine, giving it a surface examination. "Hard to say," said Max as he poked a panel on Gizmo's breastplate. "These old G2 units can be tricky. It will probably depend on what state the power unit is in. We may need to replace it, if we can, or even upgrade it."

"Even a rough guess will do for now." Mia was in no mood to hang about in the freezing cold of the museum hall any longer than she had to.

"Few hours, maybe less. Depends," said Jackie. "We'll give you a call if and when we get it going."

"Okay, but I'd like to be here when it wakes up."

Max stopped his poking around and glanced over at Mia with a look of mild incredulity on his face. "Sure, but it's just a machine. It's not like a patient coming out of a coma."

"It is to me."

"Whatever." He went back to his poking around.

Mia left them to it and headed back to her accommodation module. It was late—almost midnight, she reckoned. The corridors and walkways of this sector were deserted, since most of this area had been put into a kind of suspended animation after all the tourists had been evacuated. There was no sound except for the gentle hum of the life-support infrastructure, nothing to mark her passing, only the flicker of automatic lights as she walked.

IT WAS AROUND two hours later when Mia finally got the call. She had fallen asleep on her sofa and it took her a moment to realize it was Max, the tech, and not some MLOD emergency. She relaxed a little and tapped the side of her ear. "Yeah?"

"We're almost there with the droid. We've upgraded

the power unit... Installed a LENR instead, much better energy density and surge management. And we've run through most of the diagnostics...mainly mechanical and subsystems. Anyway, we also did a checksum on the boot sequence and primary protocols—"

Mia cut him off. "Can you just give me that in English?"

"Oh yeah, sorry... Eh, we should be ready to try for initial reactivation in twenty minutes."

"Okay, I'm on my way." She closed the comms channel and stood up. The tech sounded like it was so far so good with Gizmo, so maybe the old droid could be pressed back into service after all. *This should be interesting,* she thought as she made for the door.

When Mia arrived back at the main hall of the museum, she found Gizmo still on its low plinth with a multitude of wires and tubes snaking from its casing over to the bank of equipment the techs had brought. They were both crouched over a screen mounted on one of the trolleys, studying lines of code scrolling down the display. Jackie heard her approaching, stood up, and beckoned to her. "Hurry, the show's about to start." She pointed at the screen. "This is the last of the diagnostics. As soon as that finishes, the droid should instigate a boot sequence."

"A what?" said Mia.

"It should reactivate," answered Max.

Mia glanced at the little robot. It looked exactly as she had left it, aside from all the cables the techs had attached.

"Here we go. Fingers crossed." Jackie pointed at the screen. It had finished what it was doing and was now simply blank. They all turned to look at Gizmo.

For a moment nothing happened, then it seemed to twitch and several tiny lights flickered to life on the side of its head. Its breastplate had been removed to expose a small display that now flashed to life as data began to scroll. It was booting up.

Mia moved closer just as Gizmo's head raised itself. It then seemed to do a strange dance.

"Cool," said Max. "It's running through a self-test routine, checking all its servos."

With that, the dance stopped, and Gizmo lifted an arm and waved. "Greetings, Mia. It has been...2,354 sols since I last interacted with you. I trust you are well?"

Mia gave a laugh and shook her head in amazement. "I'm fine, Gizmo. It's good to see you again."

"And you too, although I must admit I seem to be missing a considerable amount of temporal data." It swung its head to examine the two techs, who were standing stock still with their mouths open. Gizmo raised an arm and waved again. "Greetings, Earthlings."

"Holy crap," said Jackie.

"I never really understood that phrase, other than it tends to be uttered as either a statement of amazement or as a prelude to some oncoming catastrophe. I trust you are utilizing it for the former," said Gizmo.

"Holy crap," said Max.

"I told you it wasn't your typical G2 unit." Mia couldn't help but laugh at the look on the techs' faces.

The little robot now started to detach all the cables and tubes connected to it with a rapid, fluid dexterity, so much so that neither of the techs had time to react.

Gizmo rolled off the low plinth. "I detect that there has been a significant physical expansion of the colony during my sojourn in...the museum." It moved its head to take in the space around it. "I also detect a significant deterioration in the infrastructural fabric."

"Yeah, a lot has happened these last few years, Gizmo." Mia could sense that the droid was accessing and processing data at a furious rate, trying to bring itself up to speed on all that had transpired.

"It will take me some time to process all this new information, possibly several hours."

"That's okay, Gizmo. We've got plenty of time."

"Would I be correct in assuming that you have reactivated me because I may be of some assistance to you?"

Mia gave it a broad smile. "Correct. We have a mission, you and I."

"Excellent. When do we start?"

"Very soon." Mia jerked her head in the direction of the exit. "Come on, follow me. I'll explain as we go."

They moved off, leaving Max and Jackie still with their mouths open.

5

CARAVAN

Mia sat opposite Lieutenant Bret Stanton in the freight caravan, a small, fixed table dividing them. Beside it, a window afforded them a view of the passing landscape as the caravan wound its way across the Martian surface. Not that there was anything to see—just the same dense fog of brown dust that had covered the planet for the last 368 sols.

It was cramped, packed with people and goods en route to Syrtis, some twelve hundred kilometers southwest of Jezero City. Compounding Mia's sense of confinement was the need for her, and all the other passengers, to be in full EVA suits. No one was taking any chances. Even though the caravan was the safest way to travel, there was still a lot that could go wrong. Better to be prepared than caught with your pants down, so to speak, if the compartment should suddenly lose pressure.

The caravan comprised ten individual compartments, like train carriages, connected together by a flexible umbilical airlock. Each compartment was approximately ten meters long and four wide. They were each completely independent, with their own power, life support, drive train, and comms. If one should fail, then the others could compensate. Unless, of course, the failure was catastrophic, such as a hull breach. But even then, that compartment could be detached, the surviving passengers moved, and the caravan could continue on. Bret informed her that no one had died on such a journey for at least a month. Mia made absolutely sure her suit was fully resourced before she boarded.

Gizmo had parked itself in a gap between stacks of packing crates. It was still and quiet—content, Mia supposed. It had taken its six-and-a-half-year hiatus with typical unemotional detachment, like it was a perfectly normal thing, which, from the point of view of a droid, it was. But Mia couldn't help feeling that the little robot had been hard done by. She would have to stop transferring her human emotion onto it. Gizmo didn't care; it was only interested in acquiring as much data as it could on the current state of the colony, something it achieved in less than two hours. After that, it was like it had never been deactivated. The old Gizmo was back, except for the weapons—that was the only thing it seemed put out by.

They had been traveling for several hours, but progress was slow. The caravan only managed an average speed of around fifty kilometers an hour. Yet it was smooth and relatively comfortable, so Mia dozed off about an hour into the journey. She woke up some time later with the hard metal rim of her EVA suit collar digging into her neck.

"Welcome back," said Bret, looking up from his slate.

Mia rubbed her neck to ease the ache, then reflexively looked up to the rack above their seats to ensure her helmet was still there—just in case.

"How long was I out?"

Bret lowered his slate momentarily. "Only around an hour. Still a long way to go." He gave an apologetic grin. "I've been going over some of the crime stats from the MLOD in Syrtis for the last six months."

"I can't imagine that makes for pleasant reading."

"If you think Jezero is bad, this is a lot worse." He pointed down at the slate. "We're talking riots—organized riots. We're talking major social unrest orchestrated by subversive factions within Syrtis. This goes way beyond simple crimes of the desperate and the needy."

Mia shrugged. "So what? We know all this. There's nothing new in any of that."

Bret gave a furtive glance around the compartment, then leaned in a little across the small table. He had a concerned look on his face. He kept his voice low. "This is all political, powerful industries in Syrtis vying for control."

"Not our problem, Bret. Our job is to pick up a body and return home."

Bret looked a little surprised at Mia's reaction. "But

this is a murder investigation we're on." His voice was almost a whisper.

"Only if we find some evidence to indicate that a murder has taken place. And what do you think is the likelihood of us finding any?"

Bret thought for a moment, then his face took on a resigned look. "Slim to none."

"Exactly. When we get there, the MLOD will be all professional and polite with us, while at the same time giving us the runaround until we have no option but to pack it in and head back."

"But you're still going to try...aren't you?"

Mia didn't reply, just gave him a look as if to say *What do you think?*

It was clear that Bret wasn't sure if he was reading her right. "But, the droid. You reactivated it so it could help us."

Mia rubbed her neck again; she was getting tired of dealing with Bret's naiveté. "True. But in reality, I've been waiting for an opportunity to present itself so that I could get Gizmo out of jail, so to speak. And this was it." She looked over at the robot. "We go back a bit, me and that droid. We have history together. And it saved my ass more than once, so I owe it one—that's all."

Bret sat back, a little deflated. "So, you're saying that we do nothing. Just leave it be, walk away?"

"No, I'm not saying that." Her voice was calm and measured. "All I'm saying is you need to be realistic about what we can achieve. We'll be a long way from home, and any authority that our badge affords us in Jezero City will be all but useless to us in Syrtis."

Bret was quiet for a moment as Mia's words began to sink in. "It doesn't seem fair, does it?"

"Fair? What's fair in this place?" Mia waved a hand at the dense fog outside. "It's just survival, Bret. That's all there is left for us here."

He glanced out the window for a moment, contemplating the thick brown dust. "Do you ever regret coming here?"

Mia shrugged. "There probably isn't a human living on Mars now that doesn't."

"That's not true." He looked genuinely offended by this statement.

"It's true for a lot of people." She considered him for a moment. "I'll tell you something, Bret. If I manage to survive this goddamn dust storm, you know what I'm going to do?"

He shook his head.

"Take the first ship off this godforsaken rock and get my ass back to Earth. I never should have left."

6

SYRTIS

It seemed to take forever for the caravan to dock in Syrtis. They had been waiting at the terminal for over an hour while engineers worked to secure the umbilicals, allowing the passengers to disembark. But they had problems with the seals; dust and sand had accumulated around the mechanisms, making it difficult to maintain an airtight connection. At one point, a decompression alert flashed momentarily, sending everybody scrambling for their EVA suit helmets. Eventually, two of the forward airlocks were made operational, and slowly the occupants of the caravan filed out onto the busy terminal platform.

The concourse was wide and spacious, but had a decidedly dilapidated feel to it. Illumination was poor, making it hard to get a sense of its actual size. It was busy with people milling around, some waiting to meet those who had just arrived, while some were laborers waiting for all the passengers to disembark so they could start unloading goods out of the caravan. There were also several brightly lit stalls selling food and drinks to weary travelers, as well as several kids going person to person, selling trinkets and baubles. Intermingled with this teeming mass of humanity were well-armed security guards, constantly moving, ever alert.

They were to be met by an agent from the MLOD here in Syrtis. But as Mia and Bret scanned the concourse, there was no sign of anyone. Mia checked her wrist screen for any message from the agency. Nothing.

"Anything?" said Bret, a little fatigued from the long journey.

"Nope. Maybe they've forgotten about us. We might need to make our own way there." Mia turned around to Gizmo, who was attracting the attention of some small kids. Presumably they had never seen a droid this ancient before.

"Gizmo, can you plot a route to MLOD HQ?"

"Certainly. It is approximately seventeen minutes' journey from here, at the average human walking speed."

"Okay, if no one shows up in the next few minutes, then we should just make our own way there."

Somewhere in the dark recesses of the concourse, shouts broke out and people began to scatter as a ragged individual burst through the crowd. He was running—or rather limping, as his right leg seemed to be injured. As he struggled forward, he glanced over his shoulder at two guards who were chasing him down. One raised a plasma weapon and fired. A bolt of incandescent electrical fury hit the man square in the back and sent him flying. He landed facedown along the concourse floor and lay still, a thin filament of smoke corkscrewing up from where he had been hit. A vague tang of burning flesh permeated the air.

He was dead, no doubt about it. They had used lethal force when they could have simply stunned him. Mia studied the security guards and realized that they were not MLOD officers but corporate security with a *Montecristo Industries* insignia emblazoned on their uniforms.

"I think they just killed him." Bret nudged Mia, shock evident in his voice.

She didn't reply; she was still taking in the scene. People had already begun to go about their business, not paying any heed to the guy who had just been gunned down. She began to suspect that this might be a common occurrence in Syrtis.

Mia had been so taken up by the unfolding drama that she had not noticed a petite MLOD officer coming out of the crowd and walking toward them.

"Major Sorelli?"

Mia turned to find a very young and slightly disheveled officer extending a hand to her. Mia took it. "Yes, that's me. And this is my associate, Lieutenant Bret Stanton."

"I'm Officer Nano Wells. Sorry for the delay, but we had a fire in a local accommodation module, so things have been a bit crazy."

Mia nodded and took a quick glance back to where the two guards were now dragging the body out of the terminal. She looked back at the young officer and realized that Wells was not in the least bit perturbed by the fact that two private security guards had just gunned someone down in a public space in what passed for broad daylight in this place.

"Is this your droid?" The young officer turned her attention to Gizmo. "Jeez, things must be pretty bad in Jezero if you have to use old G2 units."

"I beg your pardon, but I am not an old G2 unit. In fact..."

Mia raised a hand to the droid. "Just leave it, Gizmo." She turned back to the young officer. "Let's get going. I really need to get out of the EVA suit as soon as possible."

Officer Nano Wells's face brightened. "Sure. This way, I have a ground car waiting."

They moved off together, passing over the very spot where the young man's life had ended just a few moments earlier.

THE TERMINAL OPENED out onto a wide, elliptical plaza bisected by a busy main thoroughfare. Everywhere was thronged with traffic and people. Mia glanced up into the overhead gloom, but could not make out the roof of the vast dome that housed this sector. It was obscured by a thick haze of fine dust. They clambered into an open-topped ground car with the MLOD insignia emblazoned on the sides. Wells tapped some commands and the car moved off autonomously, merging with the traffic.

It had been a long time since Mia visited Syrtis, so her memories were vague. Nonetheless, it was clear to her that much had changed in that time, and most of it for the worse. As they moved through an accommodation sector, Mia could see that many of the units were closed up, some were borderline derelict, and one or two even showed signs of fire damage. Along the street, people gathered in small knots and groups, on corners and in gaps, and all seemed to have an air of dejected resignation about them. All wore face masks to mitigate the effects of the contaminated air.

Mia also noticed a lot of security personnel strategically placed at intersections and around specific installations. But what piqued her interest further was that, as they moved from sector to sector through the city, the insignia the security guards wore would change, presumably signifying what group controlled what area.

They finally arrived at a low, two-story municipal building with the MLOD sign illuminated over a dilapidated portico. The car drove into an inner courtyard, finally pulling up alongside several other official vehicles. Officer Wells stepped out first and turned to face Mia. "The chief says he'll see you in a half hour, so I can show you where you can stay and get out of those EVA suits, maybe freshen up."

It was the first time Wells had spoken during the

entire journey. Mia wondered if she had been told to keep her mouth shut and say nothing.

She brought them up to two rooms on the second floor—nothing fancy, basic and utilitarian. She explained that they were generally used for temporary staff, but most of them were gone now. As Mia surveyed the room, she wondered if Dan Frazer had met his end in something similar. She would get Gizmo to analyze the room's life support, just in case.

THIRTY MINUTES LATER, Mia and Bret entered the office of the chief of police of Syrtis, one Joshua T. Becker. Mia had left Gizmo back at the rooms so that the droid could give them a thorough technical check over.

The chief was a tall, heavyset man in his fifties, with the jaded demeanor of a person who has been thoroughly worn down by life. He was sitting behind a large, nondescript desk in a room filled with the bric-a-brac of a life spent on the force. Sitting at the far end of the same desk was a civilian who went by the name of Vance Baptiste. Quite what he did, or what he was doing here, Mia didn't know.

They both stood up when Mia and Bret entered, shook hands, said their greetings, and sat back down again.

"Terrible tragedy, just terrible. Agent Frazer was a good man, one of our best. His passing is a big loss for the department." The chief rested his elbows on the desk with his hands clasped together, an earnest look on his face.

"The report says he died of CO_2 poisoning in his own accommodation module?" said Mia.

"Yeah, the scrubber failed. Just one of those things. Everything is breaking down, scarcity of parts. Ah...it's a daily battle to keep everything running." He shook his head and pursed his lips. "This dust storm is extracting a heavy price from all of us."

"Once we start getting proper shipments from Earth, things should improve all around," said Bret.

Mia couldn't be certain, but she thought she saw glances exchanged between the two men at the mention of the word *shipment*. "So, you don't think he was murdered, then?"

The chief gave a forced laugh and shook his head. "Ha... It was just an accident, could happen to any of us." And there it was again, that subtle exchange between the two men.

Mia turned to Baptiste. "And what's your interest in all of this?"

Baptiste gave the disarming smile of a practiced politician. "As a representative of quite a number of the citizenry of this great city, I feel it is my duty to be here to extend a welcome to representatives of the MLOD and Jezero." He opened his hands in a disarming fashion. "It's seldom that we have official visitors these sols. Things must be bad in Jezero. I hear you are resorting to using old G2 droids?"

Mia gave her best smile. "True, things are bad in Jezero. But not quite as bad as here, I think. We don't have private security gunning down people in public."

She noticed a distinct change in the body language of the two men.

"We simply don't have the resources here that you maintain in Jezero." The chief's tone became more accusatory. "And we have four times the population. We have to rely on the cooperation of the private sector. Without them, it would be anarchy."

"What's troubling me, chief, is that your officer, Nano Wells, didn't even bat an eyelid at this incident. Which leads me to believe that it's common practice here in Syrtis. So, correct me if I'm wrong, but it is against the law, isn't it?"

Becker responded with calm, avuncular charm. "Look, these are challenging times for all concerned. We can only do what we can with what we've got. And yes"— he waved a hand in the air—"a blind eye may be turned here and there so that the resources available to the MLOD can be used where they are most needed."

Mia considered them for a moment, then decided it was time to move on. "Very well. As you say, challenging times." She gave an accepting shrug. "If we're finished here, then we would like to see the body. And also the apartment where Agent Frazer was found."

The chief's demeanor now relaxed a little. "Certainly, by all means. I will have Officer Wells bring you to the morgue."

He stood up to signify that the meeting was now at an end, then hesitated for a beat and gave Mia and Bret a concerned look. "Just a word of advice regarding your safety here in Syrtis. Try not to let too many people know that you're from Jezero. There are some folks that could be...eh, a little antagonistic."

Mia stood up. "Antagonistic?"

"I think what the chief is trying to say"—it was Baptiste who decided to answer—"is that there are some...undesirable elements within Syrtis that have somehow gotten it into their heads that Jezero is to blame for all their troubles. I know, it's ridiculous." He waved a hand in the air. "But it's best that you're aware of it now, before you walk into something...inadvertently."

Mia wasn't quite sure if this was a genuine gesture to forewarn them of potential friction with the locals, or if it was a direct threat, warning them to not go snooping around. But she let it be. "Okay, thanks for the heads up. Now, if you don't mind, we would like to see the body."

Becker tapped at a screen on his desk. "I'll have Officer Wells escort you over."

"Thanks."

"I presume you'll be heading back with the body tomorrow?" said the chief.

"That's the plan."

"Very well, we'll make sure it is suitably stored for transport."

. . .

THEY SAID THEIR GOODBYES, left the chief's office, and followed Wells as she escorted them through a labyrinth of corridors within the MLOD HQ.

Mia's earpiece pinged; she tapped it to take the call. It was Gizmo.

"How long must I be imprisoned in this room?"

Mia sighed. "Not long. We'll be back soon. Have you made any progress with my...eh, request?"

"Of course I have. As suspected, both rooms are bugged with extensive video and audio surveillance as well as comms traffic. But do not worry, I have encrypted our channel so that this conversation is secure."

"Okay, stay put. We'll be back soon."

"I hope this is not another adventure where I have to be hidden away and act dumb?"

"Just...don't go wandering around for now, okay?"

"Very well, if you insist."

They arrived at the morgue. "Gotta go, Gizmo. Talk later." She closed the comms channel.

The room was brightly lit and stark, and it had that same clinical smell of every morgue in the solar system. They walked down a long wall of storage pods until Wells stopped and placed her palm on the small control panel beside one of the hatches. There was a momentary click, then a hum as the hatch opened and a slab slid out automatically. On it lay the body of Agent Dan Frazer.

He was naked except for an electronic tag attached to the big toe of his right foot. His skin complexion was pallid, as expected. And there were no outward signs of any physical trauma. Mia leaned in closer and checked the body in more detail, looking for any indication that he may have received an injury sufficient to cause his death. But there was none. She turned to Bret. "Give me a hand to turn him over."

The lieutenant grabbed the body on one shoulder, and between them they turned him enough for Mia to examine Frazer's back. Nothing. They let him down again and stood back a little. Mia hadn't expected to find anything; she had read the coroner's report: death by asphyxiation—not an uncommon way to die on Mars.

She turned to Wells. "Any personal effects?"

The young officer touched a button on the side of the slab and a long, shallow drawer eased out from the base. "Here you go. This is everything he had on him."

There were two lots packed in transparent plastic bags. The bigger of the two contained clothes, and the other one contained all the items found on him at the time of death.

"He was fully clothed?" Mia looked up at Wells, who seemed confused by the question.

She just shrugged. "I guess so."

"I thought he died in his sleep," said Bret. "As in, he was in bed at the time."

Wells again looked apologetic. "I don't know anything about the incident. It should all be in the report."

Mia waved a hand. "It doesn't matter." She picked up the bag of personal effects, her interest drawn to the dead agent's slate. "We're taking this with us." She turned to

Bret and nodded in the direction of the door. "I think we've seen enough. Let's get going."

THEY WALKED BACK to their rooms, but said nothing as Wells escorted them. It was only when they entered Mia's room that they got a chance to talk, but not before Gizmo filled them in on the surveillance situation.

"Finally, you have returned." Gizmo's voice came through on Mia's earpiece, as well as Bret's, whose hand instantly went up to his ear. "Do not say anything you do not want them to hear," Gizmo continued. "We may need to go someplace else if you want to talk. Or I could jam the signal, but that might alert them to us knowing that we are being monitored."

Mia nodded that she understood. She turned to Bret. "You hungry? I could use some food. Let's go find a place."

Bret nodded. "Starving. Let's go."

THEY LEFT the MLOD HQ and walked out onto the main thoroughfare. It was still daytime, so there were quite a few people around, all with masks and scarves covering their mouths and noses. A thin haze hung in the air, and Mia reckoned it would be a good idea if they did likewise, as the air quality was poor—much worse than in Jezero.

She consulted her wrist screen. "There's a place just up here. We can talk as we walk. Gizmo, any joy hacking the grid terminal in that room? Can we use it to get into their systems?"

"Limited. Most of what might be useful or interesting is quantum-encrypted. Unhackable. Even I cannot get past that."

Mia tapped a few icons on her wrist screen again. "I'm sending you some video I recorded of our conversation with the chief. There was another guy there, Vance Baptiste. Can you do a search and find out who he is and who's bankrolling him?"

THEY ARRIVED at a food hall that Wells had mentioned, popular with officers and staff from the MLOD. Bret had considered that this would be like camping out in enemy territory. But Mia dismissed his concerns. "We'll find a quiet corner and stay on comms so they don't hear Gizmo. And with these masks on, they won't be able to hear or lip read too well—assuming we're not simply being paranoid. Anyway, us being here will raise less suspicion, and it's probably best that we don't go wandering off to where the locals might not be too friendly to us Jezero types."

The food hall was spacious but dimly lit, which suited Mia's needs just fine. There was a long counter on the right as they entered, a number of customers eating along it. She also spotted a few beat-up old droids. The rest of the space was taken up by around a dozen tables, none of which seemed occupied. All eyes at the counter stopped what they were doing and looked over at them as they came in. Mia gave a friendly nod and headed for the table farthest away from the counter. They sat down and said very little as they perused a menu screen embedded in the table's surface. It was mainly noodle dishes. They made their selection and waited for the food to arrive.

"So, still think it was an unfortunate accident?" Bret was keen to get down to business. He kept his voice low.

"What I think is not the issue, Bret. It's what evidence do we have that there was foul play?"

"But—" Bret was cut short by a service droid arriving with their food. Mia took her bowl and examined it for a moment before poking at it with her chopsticks.

"What about the clothes he was wearing when he was found? They said he died in his sleep, so why was he fully clothed?" Bret seemed to think he was onto something.

"Doesn't mean anything." Mia realized she was hungry, and concentrated on getting the food into her. To her surprise it was very tasty, although probably best not to consider what might be in it. She glanced over at the counter. Now that Mia and Bret had started eating, the rest of the customers seemed to ignore them; their backs were turned, heads down, busy with their own food.

Mia reached into her rucksack and took out the plastic bag with the dead officer's effects. She tore it open, extracted the slate, and presented it to Gizmo, who had taken up a position at the end of the table, its back to the counter. "Think you could hack into this, see what's on it?"

"Certainly." The droid placed the small slate on the table, booted it up, and began to interface with the device. Mia stowed the rest of the effects back in her rucksack.

"Nothing," said Gizmo matter-of-factly. "All data has been totally erased."

"Nothing?" Bret looked shocked—in complete contrast to Mia, who was busy eating. He looked over at her, waiting for a reaction.

Mia waved her chopsticks. "I would be surprised if it *wasn't* wiped clean."

Bret leaned in. "But this proves there's something not right here."

Mia finished the last of her noodles, wiped her mouth carefully with a napkin, then pushed the empty bowl aside. "It doesn't prove anything. Who's to say Frazer didn't wipe it clean himself?"

Bret seemed taken aback by Mia's response. "Why would he do that?"

"I'm not saying he did, I'm just saying we don't know. My point, Bret, is all we have at the moment are suspicions. We're going to need more than that."

Bret considered this for a moment. "So, what now?"

"We check his accommodation module where he was found, see if anything shows up. But"—she gave a shrug —"don't hold your breath." She turned to Gizmo. "Did you dig up anything on Vance Baptiste?"

"Yes, the broad strokes are that he is the director of advocacy for Montecristo Industries, a major corporation on Mars. He is also quite political, leader of a group called The Reliance, which advocates for self-autonomy for Syrtis. There is a considerable amount of information I have been able to glean, so I have selected the most relevant documents and sent them to your slate. You can peruse them at your leisure."

Bret pushed his bowl away with a vague sense of disgust. "The whole things stinks, if you ask me."

Mia considered him for a moment. "You know, it could be that he simply killed himself, things being as they are these days."

"You mean with this eternal dust storm?"

"Some people just...lose hope, I suppose?"

Bret shook his head. "I just don't believe that."

"We should go and check out that accommodation module. Who knows, it might give us some answers."

Bret brightened a bit. "You think?"

Mia shook her head. "Not really."

7

DUNE

Mia tossed, turned, and thumped her pillow more than once as she tried to get to sleep, but it was hopeless. She stared up at the ceiling, wide awake. Outside, the sounds of Syrtis drifted in, the hum of ground cars moving along the thorough-fare below, the voices of people, some of whom sounded like they'd had too much to drink.

They had checked out Frazer's accommodation module earlier. It was a modest, three-room affair whose most striking feature was its soullessness. It was spartan to the point of being clinical. What little furniture Frazer had possessed seemed to have been chosen for utility over comfort. The only deviation from this interior design style was a small collection of books—actual paper books, a wildly expensive indulgence. One had caught her attention when she first surveyed the module, primarily because she found it stuffed down the side cushion of a battered sofa in the main living area. It was *Dune*, by Frank Herbert. Mia shoved it inside her jacket and thought no more of it.

The CO_2 scrubber had been replaced and the unit fixed since the incident, so there was no way for Mia to validate the claim that a fault in this unit caused the agent's demise. Officer Wells, who had accompanied them, kept referring to the departmental report as the definitive word on all that had transpired. The only doubt cast had been whether the unit failed all by itself, or if Frazer had tampered with it, suggesting that he might have taken his own life. She had seen this thread crop up time and time again. It was never explicitly said, but any time she dug a little deeper, it seemed to be where her inquiries led.

After giving the accommodation module a quick once-over, they decided to head back to MLOD HQ and check out Frazer's desk. Mia left Bret and Gizmo to poke around Frazer's work area and terminal while she tried to interview some of his work colleagues.

From the few she managed to find and talk to, she began to build up a picture of a guy who was much respected and admired. Where negatives were voiced, they all coalesced around him being a bit of a loner with no family and few close friends. He also seemed to have an interest in conspiracy theories, but then again, what detective didn't? But even with all that, there was still nothing there, in Mia's mind, to hint at a person who had given up on life. But, as one coworker put it, *"You never can tell, can you?"*

There was also nothing in his case load that jumped out at her. All were pretty routine and pedestrian. Mostly, it consisted of assembling evidence books for cases where the perpetrators had already been apprehended. Of those still open, several were long-term no-hopers, where no breakthrough had occurred in years. There were only three cases where he was active, and all of them looked to be crimes of opportunity by nondescript lowlifes. Nothing in any of this had the potential to endanger the life of the investigator, other than in the normal course of duty. None looked to have a motive for doing away with him.

When she and Bret finally arrived back at their rooms, they pretty much agreed that there was nothing they had found so far to suggest that Agent Dan Frazer had not simply died due to an unfortunate technical failure. There were no loose threads for Mia to pull on, no chinks of light to follow, no obvious inconsistencies in the data. So, it was with a sense of resignation that they agreed to head back to Jezero the next morning with the body, and close the case.

But as Mia lay in bed and tried to get some shut-eye, a multitude of thoughts did battle in her head as her brain rummaged through half-remembered comments and snippets of data, trying to divine some deeper truth within this mess of nebulous information. Something was bugging her, something was not right, but the more she tried to put a finger on what it was, the more elusive it became.

She stood up and strode over to the window, pulled the blind down a little with one finger, and peered outside. The window had a thin film of dust clinging to its outside surface, making the view foggy and indistinct. Dull smudges of light dotted the thoroughfare below like street lamps in fog. Mia glanced up at the domed roof that enclosed this sector of the city, but it was too dark to see that far. She let the blind go and sat down on a battered armchair, one of two provided in the room.

"Can you not sleep, Mia?" Gizmo's voice was low and soft and seemed to drift across from where the little droid had parked itself for the night. It had taken up a position in the small room close to the entrance door, like a sentinel.

"No. My mind is a jumble of thoughts that won't go away." She rubbed her face. "I keep thinking of Frazer dying in his sleep from a faulty CO_2 scrubber." She glanced around the room, as if inspecting it.

"If you are concerned about the air quality in this room, my analysis indicates is moderately good, indicative of a functioning life support system, although oxygen levels are approximately 3.6% below optimal."

Mia considered the little droid for a moment, then leaned forward slightly. "Hypothetically speaking, Gizmo, how long would I survive in this room if the scrubber failed, assuming the door was sealed?"

"I estimate the volume of this space to be around 32

cubic meters, which gives you 32,000 liters of air, with minimal CO_2. The danger level would be if that rose to around 4% of volume. Considering that you exhale 13 or so liters per hour, then that would take around 96 hours."

Mia gave Gizmo a quizzical look. "That long? Are you sure?"

"Approximately. There are lots of variables, and 4% is just the level where you start to exhibit severe physical symptoms. It would need to rise to 8% to kill you."

"But Frazer died overnight, and his accommodation module is four times the size of this room."

"Five-point-three," corrected Gizmo.

"So, a faulty scrubber couldn't have killed him—it would be too slow." Mia stood up and looked over at Gizmo, seeking confirmation of this revelation.

The droid moved out from its position and into the room, close to Mia. "You obviously didn't read the detailed technical analysis of the failure in the accident report, Mia."

She sat down again and gave Gizmo a scowl. No, she didn't read it—she'd just given it a quick glance. However, she got the feeling that if she had read it, then she wouldn't be thinking she was onto something here. "Okay, Gizmo, you got me there. So, what actually happened? And just give me the short answer—my brain is too tired for any long-winded explanations."

"It is correct to say that the scrubber failed. However, there is more to this particular item of technology than simply extracting CO_2 from the atmosphere. It also stores it. Then, when the unit cannot store any more, it regenerates itself. This regeneration process releases the trapped CO_2 by venting it into reservoir tanks for industrial use. The fault in this particular unit was that it vented the gas back into the accommodation module, rapidly increasing the CO_2 levels in the space way beyond the 8% critical level." Gizmo finished with a slight theatrical wave of one arm.

"Eh...okay, I see." Mia gave a sigh and wondered why her mind was pursuing this. She should just let it lie, go back to bed, and get her ass back to Jezero tomorrow.

She got up from the seat and moved back over to the bed, then hesitated and turned to Gizmo again. "But it could have been tampered with. I mean...that type of fault is not common, is it?"

"Yes to your first question, and no to your second. That said, death by CO_2 poisoning is a common enough occurrence on Mars."

"So it's possible?"

"What is?"

"That someone did a job on that scrubber so it would vent back into the accommodation module."

"Anything is possible, Mia. But as you have so often pointed out to me on our many adventures, that does not make it evidence."

Mia gave a long sigh. "You're right, as always."

"I will take that as a compliment."

Mia climbed back into bed. "I'm too tired for any more thinking. I'll try and get some sleep now."

"Very well." The little droid parked itself back beside the door.

MIA WOKE to a voice calling her name and a hand shaking her shoulder. She slowly opened her eyes and saw Bret standing over her. "Hey, Mia, sorry to wake you. I left it as long as I could. The freight caravan is leaving in an hour."

Mia extracted an arm and rubbed her face. "Shit."

"Here, I brought you a coffee." He held it up, then placed it on the small table by the window. "I'll get out of your way, let you get dressed." He gave her a nod and headed out.

"Okay, thanks." Mia turned her head. "Gizmo, why didn't you wake me?"

"I am not an alarm clock."

Mia sighed. "No, I suppose not, but... Aw, forget it." She sat up, rolled her legs over the side of the bed, and stood up. She felt like shit. *Coffee,* she thought, and sat down at the window seat, grabbed the coffee, and took a sip. It was lukewarm but strong, and she immediately felt her brain start to wake up. She sat for a moment, just gathering her thoughts, before it was time to head to the terminal in Syrtis and embark on the long and arduous journey back to Jezero.

She would let Poe Tarkin know that they were retuning with the body of Dan Frazer, and that there was no evidence, beyond speculation, that foul play had been involved in his untimely death. Poe would not be happy, but there was only so much Mia and Bret—and Gizmo, for that matter—could do. The MLOD here in Syrtis, while being professional and courteous in facilitating the pick-up and transportation of the dead agent, were not exactly falling over themselves to open up an inquiry into the manner of his death. As Poe suspected, without cooperation on this end, little could be accomplished.

By now she had finished dressing and Gizmo had packed up most of her things. She gave Bret a call to say she was ready and to come and meet her in the room. She sat down again at the small table by the window to wait and finish her coffee.

Still arrayed on the table were some of Frazer's personal effects. Her eye went to the book that she'd found in his accommodation module the previous night. She picked it up and turned it over to read the back cover as she sipped her coffee.

It seemed to be a story about survival on an arid, dusty planet, made increasingly difficult by the machinations of various groups fighting for control of its resources. She could see why Frazer would be interested in reading it, since it resonated with their own situation here on Mars.

It was old and well-worn, and had the look of a book that had been through many hands. Perhaps she might even read it on the caravan, a way to pass the journey.

"Shall I pack these items away for you?" said Gizmo,

referring to the personal effects. "Since I have now been relegated to the lowly office of a Lobby Boy."

"Would you rather that than stuck on the plinth back in the museum?" said Mia as she stood up to let Gizmo clear the table.

"You are saying that like it is an option." Gizmo reached out to take the book and pack it away.

"I'll hang onto this, Gizmo. I might read it on the journey back. And no, going back to the museum is not an option. Not if I have any say in the matter."

"Good. I found the entire experience extremely unfulfilling."

Mia touched her earpiece to take a call from Bret. She looked over at the little droid and nodded in the direction of the door. "Time to go."

WHEN THEY ARRIVED at the terminal, it was already busy with people and goods waiting for the caravan. It was due to leave in a half hour, which gave them plenty of time. Already, the remains of the MLOD agent, Dan Frazer, had been stored in one of the goods compartments, so all they had to do now was find a seat.

Mia and Bret had been reacquainted with their respective EVA suits, which encumbered their progress through the throng that was now boarding. Nevertheless, they pushed their way along, and after a few minutes found seats and started to get settled in. Gizmo parked itself in a gap between two other, sleeker droids on the wall opposite. They stashed their EVA suit helmets in a compartment above their seats.

Mia took the book out from a pocket and started to examine it again.

"Where did you get that?" Bret leaned across the small dividing table, trying to get a better look.

Mia held it up. "Stuck down between the cushions of a seat in Frazer's accommodation module." She handed it to him.

"*Dune*. A classic." Bret took the book, handling it like it was a sacred artifact.

"You know it?"

"Oh yes. It's set on a desolate planet with lots of people trying to screw each other over for control." He jerked his head in the direction of the window. "Not unlike this one." He turned it over. "It looks like our agent friend had expensive habits. This must be worth quite a bit. You don't see many of these old paper books around anymore." He handed it back to her. "Anyway, the story is right up your street. You'll enjoy it."

"*Twenty minutes until embarkation. Please ensure all items are stored securely,*" the disembodied announcement echoed around the compartment. Mia flicked through the pages of the book and found that it opened naturally at a point around midway through. There was a small slip of paper tucked into the crease. She pulled it out.

It was a note written in scratchy handwriting. *Meet Lloyd Allen 17:50. Could be key. MC47:63.*

"Bret, is there a character in this book with the name Lloyd Allen?"

The officer gave a slow shake of his head. "It's a very long time since I read it. Doesn't sound like one. Why?"

She showed him the paper fragment with the note.

He gave her a look as if to say, *So?*

"If this was written by Frazer, then he was meeting someone that we don't know about. Someone who knew him that we haven't talked to. Someone new."

Bret looked slightly incredulous. "That bit of paper could be fifty years old, or more. It might have just been left in there and used as a bookmark down through the ages."

"*Attention, seven minutes to embarkation. Please ensure all personal items have been stowed securely.*"

Mia jumped up, opened the overhead compartment, and pulled out her bag. She placed it on the small table and found where Gizmo had stored Frazer's personal effects. She rummaged through them and withdrew a small aluminum case. It was rectangular, about the size of her palm, and thin, maybe the width of her little finger. She pressed a button on its side and the face flipped open to reveal a neat paper notepad and a slim ink pen. Bret, seeing this, now stood up from his seat.

Mia took the pen, scribbled a swirl on the paper, tore out the sheet, and held it side by side with the note from the book. "Same paper, same pen." She offered it to Bret, who studied it closely for a moment. "He did write this, and it must have been recent."

"Possibly," said Bret. "But...it's just a name."

"*Attention. Five minutes to embarkation. Please ensure all personal items are stored securely.*"

They were now beginning to draw attention to themselves, so Mia sat back down on her seat. Bret followed suit. She tapped her earpiece to open comms with Gizmo. "Are you still connected to the data grid, Gizmo?"

"Yes, Mia, I am. I do not disconnect until we embark from the terminal."

"Good. I need you to run a search on a name, Lloyd Allen. And do it quick."

A few seconds later, Gizmo replied. "I have found public records for three individuals. One is a recent arrival from Earth, 29 years old, a bio-engineer located in Elysium. Another is an administrator, 43 years old, working for the government education department in Jezero. The last one is 48 years old, an electronics engineer and a former owner of Allen Robotics here in Syrtis."

Mia looked over at Bret, who was also listening to the results of Gizmo's search.

"I'll bet it's the last guy, the one here in Syrtis."

"It's possible," Bret replied, not sounding overly convinced.

"*Attention. One minute to embarkation.*"

Mia jumped up from her seat and reached up to the overhead compartment for her bag and helmet. "I'm going to find him and figure out what he knows."

"What?!" Bret almost shouted it out, then lowered his

voice. "We're about to leave. There's no time. What about Frazer's body? There'll be hell to pay if we're not accompanying the remains when they arrive back in Jezero."

"You stay here and accompany the body. But me and Gizmo are getting off." She was already on the move toward the door, leaving Bret with a dazed look on his face.

"Gizmo, quick—follow me. We're getting off this caravan before it leaves."

"Excellent," said the little droid. "I was wondering how long it would take before you did something crazy."

8

ATTACK

Mia stood on the terminal concourse in Syrtis, watching her ride back to Jezero City leave without her and Gizmo.

"Much as I enjoy our adventures, Mia, I am at a loss to see how this course of action could be considered a good plan." The little droid swiveled its head this way and that, studying the layout of the terminal.

"I have to admit, Gizmo, I'm wondering that very same thing." Mia was now also surveying the area. "Well, it's too late now. We're committed. There's no transport back to Jezero for another three sols, so we might as well do what we came here to do and try to find this Lloyd guy."

"I have not been able to ascertain an exact address for him from the public network. I would need access to the systems in MLOD HQ for that."

"No way we're going back there, Gizmo. We need to

try to stay under the radar, keep a low profile. I don't want them to know we're snooping around."

"I assumed that would be the MLOD's job, to snoop around."

"Yes, but this is different."

"How is it different?"

"Gizmo," Mia almost shouted, then realized and lowered her voice. "It just is, okay?"

"If you say so, but—"

"But nothing," Mia interrupted the droid, then sighed. "Look, just see if you can dig up something on the network that might be of use in tracking this guy down."

"Very well, if you insist."

"In the meantime, I need to get out of this EVA suit."

The terminal concourse had a deserted feel to it now. Gone was the hustle and bustle of earlier; only a few people remained—workers and terminal staff, mostly. They made their way to an area within the building complex that housed a temporary public storage facility where travelers could stash items for a few sols. This was mostly used for EVA suits, as these were not needed in the city, but were a mandatory requirement when taking any form of surface transport on Mars.

Mia swiped her badge over the keypad of a free unit and the door clicked open. She was taking a risk using her official ID and paying through MLOD expenses; there would be a record, a trail, a way for her to be tracked. But she reckoned that, since they assumed she was now safely on her way to Jezero, they wouldn't be looking for her just yet.

She stepped into the unit, no bigger than a small wardrobe, and clambered out of the bulky suit. As she hung it up and began to attach the various services that would now charge it and replenish the suit's resources, she queried Gizmo as to any useful information it might have managed to find in its search through the public broadcast network.

"Lloyd Allen had a small business servicing droids, rovers, and mining equipment. It operated out of a facility near the spaceport, over in the western quadrant of Syrtis. According to reports, this business operated successfully for several years, in tandem with the city's development, until a rival operation was established by Montecristo Industries."

"That's Vance Baptiste's corporation."

"Apparently Montecristo aggressively targeted Allen's clients, enticing them away. There are also some unsubstantiated rumors of intimidation of both Lloyd and his employees. This went on for several months until Montecristo finally forced his business, along with several others, to close down. After that, there is not much information. There is only one mention of him, around four months ago when he was arrested at a political demonstration and charged with inciting a riot."

"What was the demonstration about?" Mia finished storing her EVA suit and was now closing the storage compartment door.

"Nothing specific that I can see. It seemed to be an amalgam of disparate groups coalescing around the inability of the administration in Syrtis to deal with the breakdown of infrastructure due to the ongoing dust storm."

"So he's a bit of a crusader?" Mia entered a random code into the door's keypad to lock it.

"It would seem so. One interesting tidbit is that these protestors had a very negative view of Jezero City."

"I keep hearing this. Why is that?"

"The story that has gained traction is that the government of Mars in Jezero City is causing unnecessary suffering of the people by its intransigence over the concessions required by Earth-based corporations before they send increased supplies of vital spare parts and aid."

"Well that's just crap, Gizmo. Mars is being held to ransom. Just when we need Earth most, they turn around and kick us in the teeth."

"I do not profess to have an opinion either way. I am just a humble robot. The ways of humans are much too complex for my simple mind."

Mia gave the little droid a quizzical look that morphed into a smile. "I think the long rest you had in the museum has given your *simple mind* a new level of cynicism. Or maybe it's just from hanging out with me for too long."

"Perhaps both."

Mia adjusted a dust mask around her nose and mouth until it fit comfortably. Then she donned her visor and tapped her wrist pad to bring up an augmented reality view of the area. "Okay, the way I see it is we have two choices. We could find a place to stay and hole up for a few sols until the next caravan is due. In other words, forget about this crazy endeavor, just stay low and keep out of trouble. Or we could take a look at the area where Lloyd Allen had his business, snoop a little, ask a few questions, and see what happens."

"Judging by the way you are studying that augmented realty map of the industrial sector in Syrtis, it would seem you have already made up your mind."

Mia turned her head to looked at the droid. "You know me so well, Gizmo." She smiled. "Okay then, let's go make a nuisance of ourselves."

SYRTIS WAS a city whose foundation began as a mining colony. Its subsequent development mirrored that of many centers of human activity since the dawn of civilization. What started as a mining outpost soon began to suck in capital and people as the industry developed. Processing plants were built to refine the extracted ore on-site rather than incur the costs of transport to Jezero City. A new spaceport was also built to facilitate the shipping of goods back to Earth.

Syrtis soon became a hive of human activity, and like many mining hubs, a downtown started to emerge to accommodate and entertain the workers and their families. New living sectors were built, along with bio-domes for agriculture and new streets for retail and leisure. The city now housed over four hundred thousand people, not all of whom worked in the mining industry. Most now worked in the myriad of ancillary activities that fed off its primary source of wealth.

All this development and specialization served Syrtis well. But it also had the knock-on effect of denuding Jezero of its heavy industry as, one by one, these operations upped sticks and moved to Syrtis. As a result, Jezero became a more genteel place, the seat of government, a tourist destination and the city of choice on Mars, if you had the money to live there.

This perceived difference in status between the grubby city of sweat and toil and the sunny uplands of the rich and powerful became a source of much friction between the citizens. At best, this manifested itself as good-humored jibes. At worst, it had the potential to boil over into hatred and even violence. The final straw for many in Syrtis was the reluctance of the government in Jezero to concede to the demands of the Earth-based corporations, whom they relied on for vital supplies of those goods that could not be manufactured on Mars. And as the endless dust storm rolled on, eroding the very infrastructure needed for human survival, it was understandable that tempers began to flare.

All this Mia had learned since her arrival in Syrtis, perhaps not in great detail, but enough to know that they could be walking into trouble if they weren't careful. It didn't help that she was traveling with an antiquated droid. Gizmo was drawing attention from people as they passed along the main thoroughfare. Mia kept her head lowered, her eyes straight ahead, and focused on the destination marker highlighted in her AR visor.

They had decided back at the terminal to go and check out the physical location of Lloyd Allen's old business venture. It was located in a sector sandwiched between the refineries and the spaceport, designated for light industry, and was generally referred to as the maintenance sector. As they walked, Mia began to get a sense that a lot of folks in Syrtis seemed aimless, with nothing to do and no place to be. Small groups of people knotted around corners and open spaces, some sitting, some drinking, but not much else.

The route they were taking was along the main backbone that sliced through the heart of the city. Behind them lay the great agri-domes and agricultural sectors. Those led into the administrative and leisure sectors, which they were now leaving, and entering into a more industrial sector.

Mia checked her AR display. "It's not far, another six hundred meters." She stopped at a junction and looked right, down another wide thoroughfare. "Down here, on the right somewhere."

They walked past small industrial units, closed up and shuttered. There were few people and even less activity. After walking for a few minutes, Mia's AR display indicated that they should be standing right outside the old business premises of Lloyd Allen.

Mia stopped and looked around at the shuttered facility. "This should be it." She walked up to what looked to be the front door of a wide, tall, highly engineered structure, built as an airlock and big enough to accommodate large vehicles. On the wall beside it, a small sign read *Allen Robotics*. It was coated in a thin film of dust, like everywhere else in the city.

Gizmo was examining something on the entrance door.

"You got something there?" said Mia as she moved over to see what had intrigued the droid.

"No dust on the locking mechanism. And see here, along the edges of the door? No dust, either."

"Someone has been in here recently." Mia removed the AR visor to get a better look. "Or is still in there."

Mia stepped back at the realization that someone might be inside, perhaps even watching them on a monitor. She glanced around the exterior wall for signs of a camera. But even if there was one, it would be very difficult to spot.

"Do you want me to open it?" Gizmo was now examining the keypad beside the door.

"You think you can hack it?"

The little droid's head swiveled around to consider Mia. "Of course. Is that not why you had me reactivated, so that I can do whatever hacking needs to be done?"

Mia paused for a moment, then smiled and stabbed an index finger at the robot. "Like I said, Gizmo, you know me so well." She looked back at the building. "Not right now, people may have seen us come up here, and...it would be good to know if there is someone inside before we go barging in uninvited." She looked back at Gizmo. "Only one way to find out."

She walked over to the door, pressed the intercom, and waited. Nothing. She tried a few more times, putting her ear up to the door to try to hear any movement from inside. Still nothing.

"Okay, either there's no one at home, or they're hiding out. Let's try to find out a bit more before we resort to breaking and entering."

"Very well," said Gizmo. "So, what is our next step?"

Mia turned her head to face back up the route they had just taken. "We passed a bar at that last junction that looked open. I suggest we pay it a visit and ask a few questions. Maybe someone in there knows something."

THE BAR, called the Neutrino, was set a little back from one corner of the crossroads. It had some seating outside, with a few people eating. All around this junction, a number of smaller business had set up shop—small workshops, mainly—and most of their activity had spilled out onto the walkway, merging with street vendors and the general public. The area was busy and had a lively feel. It seemed to be the center of activity for this entire sector, feeding off all the people that worked in the factories and workshops in this area. All this activity had kicked up a thin haze of dust that hung in the air, softening the edges of the structures, blurring the details, so much so that the people moved as if in slow motion.

Like the rest of the businesses around the junction, the bar operated part outside and part inside; there was no door as such, just an indistinct transition. The term *outside* was something of a loose term on Mars, as, strictly speaking, outside meant the surface, beyond the structures of the city.

Mia glanced up at the curved, transparent roof of the thoroughfare. In normal times, this would provide ample light to the people below. But these were not normal times; all she could see was the dense, brown haze of the ever-present dust storm darkening the sky and casting a dim, pale light onto the street below.

They made their way into the dull interior of the bar, which was clearly designed for utility rather than ambiance. Everything in it—the counter, the walls, the tables and chairs—all seemed to be made of the same dull beige material. It had the feel of a medical clinic whose surfaces had become cracked and yellowed with age.

A few tables were occupied with customers, all of whom were avidly watching a public broadcast on a large screen at the back of the bar. It looked to be a news story of an incident somewhere in the city. They made their way to the bar counter and Mia parked herself on a hard, plastic stool. The barman took his eyes away from the broadcast and looked them over. He was tall and heavy-set, dressed in a dull, brown overall with the sleeves torn off. Around his mouth and nose he wore a complex dust mask that had the look of handcrafted industrial salvage.

He shifted his bulk from his elbows and came over with a nod. "What'll it be?"

"Eh...I could use a coffee?"

His response was unmoving. Instead, he gave her a curious look, then glanced at Gizmo. "That's an old G2 unit, if I'm not mistaken. Haven't seen one of those in a while."

"I am not a G2 unit. I—"

Mia raised a hand to Gizmo to stop it from talking. "Eh, yeah, it's...a version of one."

The barman studied them for a beat, then turned to get Mia's coffee. While his back was turned, Mia poked a finger at Gizmo and whispered, "Don't even think about talking."

The little droid shifted slightly, but said nothing.

The barman returned with the coffee presented in a plastic mug in a similar shade of dull beige as the rest of the decor. He leaned in a little across the counter. "I take it you're not from around here?"

Mia didn't reply. Instead, she took a sip of coffee and concentrated on looking at the counter long enough for the question to drift away. She clasped the mug in both hands and looked back at the barman when she was satisfied that he wasn't going to pursue the query. "Say...that unit down there at the end of the street, Allen Robotics. I don't suppose you know where I could find the owner, Lloyd?"

He stepped back a bit from the counter, gave her a suspicious look, and folded his arms. "And who wants to know?"

"I'm a friend of a friend."

"Is that so. You wouldn't be MLOD, would you?" With the mention of this, Mia could sense a change in vibe in the bar. Gizmo started to twitch—never a good sign. She glanced over her shoulder to find a few of the customers now taking an interest in them.

She turned back to the barman. "Lloyd Allen. Do you know him?"

"Nope." He glanced up at the screen. Something showed up that seemed to get the rest of the customers a little agitated. There were heated words being flung at the screen.

Mia jerked her head in the direction of the broadcast. "What's the story?"

"Incident down at sector twenty-five. Primary oxygenator failure. Sector is sealed off, looks like multiple deaths. Bad... Very bad." He kept his eyes on the screen as he spoke.

"This damn storm," said Mia. "It's killing us all."

He turned back to Mia. "For sure. Listen, who did you say you were?"

Mia sensed he might be softening a bit now that she had let him know that they were all in this together, so to speak. So, she took a chance. "I'm investigating a...possible murder."

The barman raised an eyebrow.

"Dan Frazer. He was an MLOD agent. They say he died in an accident, a CO_2 scrubber malfunction, but I don't think so. Before he died, he was meeting with Allen. That's why I want to talk to him. Find out what he knows."

The barman considered her for a moment. "So, you are MLOD. But you're not from around here, are you?"

"No, I've come over from Jezero." As soon as she said it, she felt as if the bar had just experienced rapid decompression. Everything froze; she felt fingers of ice spread their tendrils across every surface in the room. She had just said the wrong thing, to the wrong people, at the wrong time.

The barman leaned in and slowly took her mug away. "The coffee was on the house," he said in a low voice. "Now I think it's time you left."

Mia stared at him for a moment. She knew the score; she had just stepped on a landmine, and her best course of action at this very moment was to not make any sudden moves. She nodded slowly, stepped off the stool, and started for the street.

She glanced back to check the lay of the land, see if anyone was getting twitchy—always good to know what's going on when your back is turned. The customers were all standing and facing her; their body language spoke of threat. Then they started to inch their way toward her. Mia considered reaching for her pistol, but reckoned it might be the very excuse they needed.

The barman came out from behind the counter in a

fluid, purposeful motion and placed himself between Mia and the mob of customers. He raised a hand to them. "Go back to your food. She's leaving, party's over." He moved over to Mia, took her elbow in one hand, and gently got her outside. He walked her a few meters until they were out of sight of the crowd inside. Then he turned to her. "You want to know about Lloyd?"

Mia nodded. "Yes."

He glanced up and down the street, then whispered to her, "Take the next right, up there." He pointed. "Around two hundred meters, there's a small service corridor on the left. I'll meet you there in ten minutes. Now go... Go!"

Mia and Gizmo moved with purpose. "That was tense," said Mia after she felt she had gotten far enough away from the bar.

"They do not like people from Jezero. Very irrational."

"Well, that's humans for you. They convince themselves of all sorts of things that have no basis in reality."

"Like you thinking that Agent Dan Frazer was murdered?"

Mia stopped and looked at Gizmo for a moment. "Yeah, I suppose so. It's really just a hunch. Anyway, we might get something out of this barman."

"My analysis of the situation suggests that it could simply be a trap."

"I know. That's my guess, too, but it's the only lead we have." Mia unzipped the front of her jacket, pulled out the plasma pistol, and checked it to make sure it was ready for action.

"This is it. This is the place he wanted to meet at." Mia glanced down the narrow corridor. It wasn't very deep, maybe twenty meters. Small doors punctuated the walls, rear entrances to the industrial units on either side—all closed, presumably locked. It was deserted. "Not a good place to get trapped," said Mia as she looked around. "And we're a bit early. Maybe we should go and wait somewhere else first?"

The attack was sudden, and came from precisely where Mia wasn't looking—above her head. It felt like she had been hit by a falling shuttle engine. Someone had been following them along the rooftops and had now pounced down on her. He caught her on her shoulder and upper back as he dropped down, and she folded like a marionette with its strings cut. Her face was smashed into the floor, a heavy knee dug into her back, and a strong hand grabbed her hair at the back of her head and repeatedly slammed her face back down on the ground. She screamed in pain, trying to wriggle enough to get at her pistol.

"Bitch. Think you can swan in here from Jezero and start poking around like you own the place?" Mia thought she recognized the voice as one of the people at the bar.

She twisted and turned and managed to extract the pistol enough to try to take a shot. She fired off blindly, not looking to really hit anything—it was simply an action designed to give her some room to maneuver. She felt the hand on the back of her head release its grip, and she immediately looked around, trying to find a proper target.

She could see Gizmo was besieged by three assailants armed with heavy metal tools, bashing and beating at it. One assailant was using a long metal bar which Gizmo had managed to grab in one arm, but the assailant was hanging on. Two others were behind the droid, hammering its head and shoulder. Gizmo took a massive hit, and something seemed to give around its neck; its head tilted awkwardly to one side, and the arm holding the metal bar lost power. It hung limp and released the bar, freeing it up to be used against it.

Mia witnessed all this in the instant it took her to aim in the general direction of her attacker, still pressing on her back. But he sensed the threat, shifted quickly, and a heavy boot landed on her wrist. The shot cracked and fizzled off the side wall of the corridor.

"Bitch," she heard him say as the pistol was violently kicked out of her hand. Mia screamed in pain, and again as another kick connected with her lower ribcage.

"Stop!" a new voice shouted out above the melee, and there was a momentary pause in the assault. Mia craned her neck to locate its source. A tall, thin, elegant man strode up the corridor toward them, a hand held in the air. The group attacking Mia and Gizmo must have known him, as they all stood still, just looking at him.

The attacker raised an arm and pointed an accusatory

finger at the advancing figure. "Stay out of this. You don't need to get involved."

"Is this how you deal with your anger, by beating up anyone from Jezero? And how's that going to do any good?" The man moved to within a meter of the group.

"These bastards need to know we don't want them around, after what they're doing to us," the attacker continued.

It was now the man's turn to poke an accusatory finger. "You leave them be, or so help me, I will never fix any of your shit for you ever again." He swung around to look at the others. "That goes for the rest of you. Next time your oxygenator or scrubber breaks down, don't come crying to me."

Mia realized that this man's power came from his knowledge, his technical abilities. In the land of the blind, the one-eyed man is king, and within this group, he was the one who had the skills they all relied on to keep the lights on, the oxygen generating, and the filters working. Without him and his abilities, life would get a lot more difficult for them.

There was a moment's pause as his threat began to sink in. He pressed home his advantage. "I mean it. You can all go somewhere else and pay for fixing your shit. So, you leave them be, you hear?"

The group grumbled as they glanced at each other. This man was respected, and his threat was obviously a big deal. The attacker looked down at Mia, then gave her another kick, followed by a gob of spit that splattered on the side of her face. "Don't come around here again. You might not be so lucky the next time." He walked off, and his group followed behind.

Mia slowly shifted her body so she could sit and rest her back against the wall.

The man approached her and knelt to examine her. "You okay?"

"Not really. I think I might have a broken rib." She grimaced as she felt her left side.

The man stood up and jerked a thumb over his shoulder. "My place is not far. Let's get you sorted out." He extended a hand to help her up.

"Who are you?" said Mia as she got herself vertical.

"Lloyd Allen. Most people just call me Lloyd." Mia's shock at the mention of his name must have registered with him, as he raised a hand and nodded. "Yeah, I know. I heard some MLOD officer from Jezero was looking for me, asking about Agent Dan Frazer. Thought I'd go look for you before those morons from the bar took their frustrations out on you." He waved a dismissive hand. "Believe it or not, they're not the worst. This is a dangerous part of town to go poking around in. You need to be careful turning over a rock here—you never know what will crawl out from under it."

"Thanks," Mia managed, then looked over at Gizmo. The droid had taken a beating. One arm had been dislocated at the shoulder joint, and its head hung at an odd angle. But it was still functioning. "Gizmo, how bad are you? Can you move?"

"I am not liking this place very much." Its head moved to right itself, but seemed to grind and squeak as it did.

"Me neither."

Lloyd inspected the droid. "I think I can fix that. Come, let's get off the street. Then we can talk."

_____

9

ALLEN ROBOTICS

M ia presumed that Lloyd was taking them to an accommodation module somewhere on the periphery of the maintenance sector. What she was not expecting was to be ushered into a vast, cluttered warehouse space only a short distance from where they had been attacked.

The interior could only be described as ordered chaos, a kind of scrapyard with zones, like some war-ravaged city where the general tenor of each sector could just about be understood. There were several long lines of machines for metalwork, others for the more delicate electronics work, and other, more esoteric tech whose purpose was beyond Mia's capacity to comprehend.

Scattered around this central workshop core were the disemboweled carcasses of a great many machines: droids, drones, transport pods, life-support systems. There were even several rovers of varying size parked way at the back. And, if her eyes didn't deceive her, at least one small shuttle.

"Holy crap, is all this yours?"

Lloyd gave a nonchalant gesture with his head. "Yeah, some of it."

"You mean there's more?"

"Used to be a lot more, but this is some of what remains." He waved an arm around the space.

Mia had learned something of Lloyd's background on the short journey from the site of the mugging that she and Gizmo had just received. He told her that he had set up a shuttle and robotics maintenance business many years ago. It went well for a time, but then Montecristo Industries moved in when the entire industrial area was undergoing massive expansion. They undercut the locals, the smaller business, and slowly pushed them out as the businesses found it impossible to compete. He himself was one of the last to close, eight months ago. He laid off over a hundred workers, closed, and sold off most of his holdings to Montecristo, but kept this place, mainly because he simply did not want to part with all the stuff he had accumulated.

Since then, he had been doing some maintenance work for free, mostly for those in this area who were unemployed, let go by the many business that had closed down. They had little or no money. Most lived by scavenging, doing what they could; barter was their currency, and Lloyd had built up a large cohort of people who owed him one. It also struck Mia that he had, at some point, been quite wealthy, most of which was gone now, but he still had a lot more than most.

"Come, this way. Let's get you seen to." He threaded them through rows of machinery, crates of spare parts, and the carcasses of half-assembled machines to a walled-off section in the vast warehouse. They entered through a wide, open set of doors into a more intimate space. This was where he lived, Mia presumed. The ceiling was low, the lighting dim save for a long bench along the back wall that hosted an impressive array of technical equipment for the service and repair of electronics. Long, bright strip lights hung low over the bench, and Mia could see several units being worked on.

The rest of the space was filled with a myriad of domestic and personal effects—too many to take in in one quick glance around. The center of the space had three battered sofas around a low table fashioned from the escape-hatch door of a standard transport shuttle. The rest of the decor were equally upcycled parts from some machine or other.

"Sit. I'll get a med-kit."

Mia lowered her battered body onto one of the sofas. It was so low that she feared, with all the pain her body was experiencing, she would struggle to get up from it again. Her ribcage was the source of most of her trauma; it hurt when she breathed. Her left side was bruised and bloodied, but she didn't think now that anything was broken. As for her face, the right side hurt like hell since it had been smashed into the ground during the attack.

She was afraid to look in a mirror for fear of what she might find.

Gizmo parked itself near the door. It had not spoken much since the attack—unusual behavior as Mia normally had trouble getting it to shut up. But perhaps it had finally taken heed of her requests for it to not say much to anyone, in case they start to get suspicious of the droid and have it reveal itself as a lot smarter than the average G2 unit. So maybe that was it, or maybe it was just being sullen after getting a good beating. Either way, Lloyd had not given Gizmo so much as a quick look-over, presuming it to be just an old, rudimentary service robot.

He returned with a small pack of medical supplies, along with a bowl of warm water and some towels. They went to work checking her over, cleaning her up. They talked.

"So how do you know Dan Frazer?" asked Mia as she wiped the blood from her face.

"I don't. At least, we never met. We just messaged once, and that was to arrange to meet."

"What about?"

He stood up, walked over to the long workbench, and started rummaging around in a drawer. "Let me show you. I have it here somewhere."

Mia had by now managed to clean up most of the cuts on her face. It felt much worse than it looked, but she did have a gash on her temple. Her right hand had been bandaged, but as for her ribcage, there was not much she could do about that other than try not to breathe.

"Have a look at this." He handed her a small, flat, square object, vacuum-packed in translucent plastic. It was small enough to fit in her palm.

Mia examined it. "Microprocessor?" She turned it over.

"Correct. The most valuable thing, by weight, on Mars. This is one of the new breed of radiation-hardened chips specifically designed for our current situation on Mars. It's made on Earth. But look at the date of manufacture on the package."

Mia turned it over and read the small print etched into the packaging. "This was fabricated four months ago, so it must have arrived on Mars within the last few weeks." Mia looked back at Lloyd. "Part of an aid shipment?"

"Yes, but I got this one on the black market. And the guy I got it from says there's a lot more where that came from. He didn't say exactly where he got it. But he does work for Montecristo Industries. So, my suspicion is that they are siphoning off inventory from the aid shipments. In fact, I'm pretty sure of it."

"Have you any proof of this?"

He shook his head. "No. But through my contacts I found out that Agent Frazer was investigating a black-market operation involving stolen components. So, I contacted him and told him about my theories. I thought we might be able to help each other."

"And now he's dead."

Lloyd gave a resigned nod. "And now he's dead."

They looked at each other for a moment without speaking. In the background, Mia could hear a machine starting up, out on the hangar floor somewhere. Lloyd jumped up, going into high alert.

"What's that?" Mia was also getting to her feet.

"Where's your droid?"

Mia looked over to where Gizmo had parked itself earlier. It was gone.

"Gizmo," she shouted as they both moved in unison back out into the main warehouse space, where the machine noise was coming from. Mia deftly took out her plasma pistol and held it down by her side. Lloyd moved in behind her as they slowly zoned in on the source of the noise.

"Sounds like one of the CNC machines has started up."

Mia inched her way around a tall stack of crates and peered around. Then she immediately relaxed. "Gizmo, what are you doing? You scared the crap out of us." She came out from around the crates and put her pistol away.

Gizmo was working at a complex-looking milling machine. It stopped what it was doing, turned to face Mia and Lloyd, and waved with its good arm. Its other arm was missing. "My sincerest apologies. I did not mean to startle you."

It turned to gesture at the machine. "I decided, since we seem to be relatively safe here, and since you were being refurbished, that I would take the opportunity to do likewise and avail these machines of parts to put myself back together." It reached into the belly of the machine, extracted a newly fabricated component, and examined it. "Excellent tolerance. Less than a micron."

Mia looked back at Lloyd. "Sorry about this. Gizmo can be...unpredictable at times."

Lloyd didn't reply. His face was too busy looking stunned, and it took a moment for it to start responding to instructions from his brain. "That is not a G2 unit, is it?"

"Eh...no, not in the strict sense of the word. It's eh...something else."

Lloyd suddenly snapped to life and turned to Mia. "There was a droid by the same name, built a long time ago, before sentience was outlawed..." He started moving closer to where Gizmo was working. "Built by one of the founders, Nills Langthorp..." His voice trailed off as he stood and watched Gizmo reassemble its arm.

Lloyd turned back to Mia. "But it can't be. I heard it was decommissioned and ended up in a museum over in Jezero."

"You are correct on both counts," said the little droid as it tested the articulation of its reassembled arm. "But my dear friend Mia rescued me from oblivion. It would seem that desperate times require desperate acts, and my rehabilitation back into full operation was one of those. Not that I am complaining." Gizmo examined his handi-work. "Excellent."

It looked over at Lloyd. "Perhaps you would be so kind as to help me with these neck servos. I am having diffi-culty assessing the extent of the damage."

"Eh... Sure, of course. I would consider it an honor." He moved closer and started to examine the droid's neck joints. "Ah...there's your problem." He poked a finger deeper into the mechanism. "Sheared actuator shaft. Chrome vanadium, if I'm not mistaken. You must have taken quite a bashing to break that."

Mia raised a hand. "Listen, Lloyd, are we safe here for a while?"

"Absolutely. I've put the place on lockdown. Nothing is coming in here that we don't want."

"Good. Then if you don't mind, I need to rest. I'm feeling a bit...shell-shocked."

Lloyd looked concerned that he had not considered this. "Of course, I should have thought about that." He tapped his wrist screen and called one of his two service droids, Bumble and Bee. "Bee will show you where you can put your head down." He gestured back down along the row of machines to where the droid, Bee, was now coming toward them.

"Mia, are you feeling okay?" It was Gizmo's turn to express concern.

"Fine, just the painkillers kicking in. I'll be okay after an hour or two." She turned and follow Bee, leaving Lloyd to indulge his technical fascination with the droid.

10

———

COMPONENTS

Mia awoke sometime later with a fuzzy head and the sound of muffled voices coming from the floor below. Bee had taken her to a room on the second floor of the living area populated by three sets of bunk beds, probably used for workers coming off shift back when this place was in business. She rolled off one of the lower bunks that she had taken refuge on. The ache in her side had dulled somewhat. She flexed her right hand, testing it for pain. It was minimal, so she unwrapped the bandage and got to her feet.

The voices grew louder as she descended the metal staircase. Mia recognized one as Gizmo, relating a story to Lloyd.

"—so that was when I turned to the other droid and said, *'Rationalize this.'* Then blew it into smithereens with a blast from my plasma cannon."

Mia arrived in the main living area just in time to see Lloyd creased over with laughter. "Seriously?"

He was with three other people, one of whom Mia recognized as the barman from the Neutrino. They were all armed with light pulse weapons. She stiffened, considering if this was a potential threat. But the mood was jovial, and they seemed more interested in hearing Gizmo's story than in her.

"Absolutely." Gizmo pointed to its right shoulder. "I used to have one mounted here. But they took it away, along with all my other weapons."

"I can see how they might be a little uncomfortable with a sentient droid armed to the teeth." Lloyd then realized Mia had walked into the living area. "Ahh...Mia, you're awake. Good."

She eyed the newcomers suspiciously. Lloyd, sensing her discomfort, quickly introduced everyone. "I took the liberty of gathering a few like-minded friends while you were resting." He gestured at the individuals seated around. "Marcus, whom I think you already know from the bar."

Marcus gave her a nod. "Sorry about the patrons roughing you up. I wasn't quick enough getting you out of there. Don't pay them any heed—they're just shit for brains."

Mia gave him a casual nod by way of acknowledgment.

"This is Anka and Milo," Lloyd continued. "We got word that Montecristo's security activity has increased in this sector. Multiple units making clandestine incursions." He gave Mia a concerned look. "We think they're looking for you. Hence my decision to call in some backup." He gestured at the group. "Needless to say, we all share the same disdain for Montecristo and their methods." There was a collective grunting of approval around the room.

"They know I'm here?" said Mia as she sat down on a battered sofa.

"News travels fast around here. An MLOD officer asking questions about Agent Frazer has obviously got them spooked. Which leads us to believe that he must have been onto something."

Mia eyed the coffee pot on the table and pointed at it. "Is that hot?"

"Eh...no." Lloyd stood up. "Come, let's get you a fresh brew." He jerked his head toward the kitchen, indicating for Mia to follow.

Once they were out of earshot of the others, Mia got straight to the point. "Can we trust these guys? I got the impression that they had an intense dislike for anyone from Jezero."

"They're not like that. Those guys that attacked you are morons. They soak up all the bullshit that they hear without thinking. Not much up here." He tapped the side of his head. "Marcus and his crew are like me. They see what Montecristo are trying to do—take over all the sectors in Syrtis, take control. And they see it as their duty to the people of this sector to stop them."

"So, they're vigilantes?"

Lloyd cocked an eyebrow at her. "In a sense, yes. But you have to understand, most citizens see the MLOD as being in the pocket of Montecristo, so there's not a lot of faith in the system." He grabbed the freshly brewed coffee pot and poured her a mug. "Trust me, these guys are on our side."

Mia took a sip and felt herself relax a little. She rested her back against the kitchen countertop, folded one arm while holding the mug in the other, and gave Lloyd a considered look. "And what side is that, exactly?"

"The side of the people who live and work here on this planet. The ordinary people who're simply trying to survive. Not the corporations who just see us as pawns in some power game, as bargaining chips—or worse, as simply disposable." He jabbed an index finger at her. "That side. That's the one we're on."

They considered each other for a beat. Mia took another sip of coffee and then reached into an inside pocket of her jacket and pulled out the book she had found in Frazer's accommodation module. She put the coffee back down on the counter and opened the book to where she kept Frazer's note. She pulled it out and handed it to Lloyd. "This is how I knew to look for you."

He studied the scribbles for a moment.

"Dan Frazer's place had been cleaned out when I got there, but I found this stuffed down the side of a sofa. They must have missed it. I don't suppose you might know what the numbers *MC47:63* mean?"

Lloyd considered the scrap of paper for a moment. "I do. He must have written this down after I contacted him. It's a location code, used internally by Montecristo. It gives the location of a waystation out by the old shuttle port."

"Leighton?" said Mia.

"Yes, that's the one. It has grown a great deal in the last few decades since it's on a major transport route. There are a lot of storage and logistics facilities there now, so the resident population has grown, too. It's like a small town. Anyway, that component I showed you, I got it from Marcus, the barman from the Neutrino." He jerked a thumb in the direction of the living area. "And he got it from some guy who came into the bar hard up for cash. According to Marcus, he kept saying there was plenty more where that came from over at Leighton. So, I passed this information on to Frazer when we were arranging to meet."

Mia looked out to the living area, where Gizmo had resumed entertaining the vigilantes with a new story. "Let's go talk to Marcus. Maybe there's more to this."

Mia took a seat on the battered sofa opposite the barman and his crew. She sipped her coffee in silence as Gizmo finished its story of when it went on a high-speed dash across the planet surface, carrying Mia as her air ran out, trying to make it before she died. By the time Gizmo was finished, the others looked at Mia with a new kind of fascinated admiration.

"Lloyd says you...acquired this component." Mia directed her question to the barman.

"Yeah. He was kinda a goofy guy, says there's more over at Leighton."

Mia put her empty coffee mug down on the low table and sat back. "See, here's the thing I don't get. If you can get a few vital components on the black market, these would help you keep things going, keep the lights on. So what if Montecristo is bringing them in, even if they are complete bastards?"

An awkward silence followed as each of them looked to one another, wondering what game Mia was playing. Eventually, Marcus poked a finger in her direction. "Whose side are you on here?"

Mia sat up and gave him a hard look. "I'm on the side that wants to find out if Agent Dan Frazer was murdered, and if so, who killed him."

"Well, let me explain why we give a shit." Lloyd raised a hand. "If Montecristo has been stockpiling vital components, siphoning off from the aid supplies, or sidelining the embargo, these could have been used to prevent multiple disasters. Every day there are systems breaking down, people dying, all because of the lack of vital components that they've taken out of circulation and stashed somewhere. The reason we care,"—he gestured with both arms—"the reason anyone cares, is because people are needlessly dying while Montecristo plays power games."

Mia sat back and considered the group, then nodded. "Okay, I hear you."

There was an immediate relaxation in the room, the mood softening. "You don't much trust folk, do you?" said Anka, finally.

"Don't take it personally. It's just part of the job." Mia sat up again, resting her arms on her thighs, clasping her hands together. "While I was in MLOD HQ, I read through all of Frazer's case files, and there was no mention of Montecristo, no mention of an investigation he might have been conducting. Now that's not to say he wasn't doing any—he may have kept the whole thing on the quiet—but I do remember several mentions of Leighton waystation. In fact, he was over there three sols before he died. It seems to me that all roads now lead to this waystation. So, I need to get in there and take a look around."

"Yeah, agreed," said Lloyd. "We've been giving that a considerable amount of thought. It's not going to be easy to get in there. For one, it's over three kilometers outside the city, so the only way to get there is by rover. And with this never-ending dust storm, all surface activity is strictly controlled."

"Unless you can wave your badge and commandeer one?" said Milo, half joking.

"Theoretically, I could try that, but that's just going to announce my arrival. No, we need a way to sneak in unseen. What about the rovers I saw at the back of your workshop?"

"Not working. They've been scavenged for parts for other machines."

"Could we get one working?" Mia continued.

Lloyd scratched his chin. "Possible, but we still need to find parts, and even then it could take a while."

"There must be some back-and-forth traffic from Leighton to Syrtis?"

"Yeah, but it's all Montecristo small transports. Nowhere to hide in them."

"Even if we do get a rover working, there's the problem of navigation in this cursed storm. It would be easy to get completely lost."

"Not for me," said Gizmo. "I could navigate there with 98.37% accuracy, storm or no storm."

They all looked at the droid for a moment. Nobody doubted it could do it.

"Well," said Lloyd finally, "at least that solves that problem."

"We'll need a detailed schematic of the entire waystation so we can look for a way in with the lowest risk of being spotted," said Mia. "Also, it might give us some idea of where they could be stashing the components."

"Yes, we can get that," said Lloyd.

"That goofy guy comes into the bar every other sol," said Marcus. "I can try and pump him for some intel on where they might be stored."

"Good," said Lloyd. "In the meantime, I'll get started on the rover, see what it needs."

Mia considered that now might be a good time to

brew up some more coffee, since the effect of the last one had worn off. She rose from the sofa and was just about to head for the kitchen when several alerts blared out from all around the living area.

"What the hell is that?" Mia looked around, trying to find their source.

Lloyd was already on his feet, rushing over to the bench with all the monitors. He flipped on a holo-table showing a schematic of the warehouse and the surrounding area. Clumps of red dots pulsed at different locations.

"Security. Shit, they know you're here. I think they're planning a raid."

By now, the others had grabbed their weapons and were frantically checking them.

"You need to get out of here." Lloyd's face twisted into an amalgam of fear and urgency.

Mia looked to Gizmo, who had moved in beside her, sensing the urgency of the situation, then back to Lloyd. "How?"

"Not out the front." Lloyd pointed at the 3D schematic on the holo-table. "They've got the area covered. They'll nail you if you try that." He flipped on a couple camera feeds, and they could see several groups of Montecristo security personnel advancing along both sides of the street outside.

"Shit," said Marcus. "We'll never shoot our way through that."

"The surface," Lloyd shouted at Mia. "You gotta get out

onto the surface. That's the only way. We'll stay here—they're not after us. It's you they want."

"What? You mean EVA into the storm at night? It'll be pitch black out there."

"Lloyd is right," said Gizmo. "That is our best chance. They did not consider the outside surface as an option. That is why there is no security out there. I can navigate."

"Great idea," said Mia, a little sarcastically. "Only problem is, I don't have my EVA suit, remember? I left it in the locker at the terminal."

"I've got some," said Lloyd. "Quick, this way. We don't have much time."

"Lloyd, you better see this." Anka was pointing at one of the camera feeds. "They've brought some serious heavy weaponry with them."

Mia glanced at the feed. In the hazy picture, she could just make out an autonomous robotic quadruped moving stealthily behind the main group of security personnel, and there was no mistaking the heavy battering ram mounted on its back.

"You need to get going." Lloyd grabbed Mia by the elbow and bundled her out of the living area and into the workshop area. "Down the back. Through that door." He pointed as he ran. "Hurry."

A deep, resonant boom echoed around the cavernous space. "Shit, they're trying to ram down the entrance doors."

Mia heard it again as they charged into the rear of the workshop, dodging between all manner of vehicles in varying states of disassembly. They headed for the back wall, which consisted of one massive airlock for getting rovers in and out. She heard the same booming sound again. It was more muffled this time, but it still sounded like they had not broken through yet.

Lloyd frantically checked through a locker full of EVA suits. They all had a distinct industrial design, and looked old and battered. Mia hoped he'd find one that wasn't going to clap out after ten minutes on the surface.

"Here." He lifted a suit down from its hanger. "It's good for around four hours."

Another boom. But this time it sounded different, like the doors were about to collapse. She wasted no time in getting suited up. It was basic, nothing fancy, but if it kept her alive, that was all that mattered.

She snapped on the helmet, lifted the visor open, and ran through the boot-up sequence as Lloyd operated the controls to open the inner airlock doors. When the gap was wide enough, Mia and Gizmo squeezed through just as another boom was followed by an almighty crash that resonated throughout the entire structure.

"They must be through." Lloyd slapped the button to close the airlock door and pulled out his plasma pistol. "It's time to go. Good luck."

The door shut just as Mia snapped her suit visor down. "Gizmo, can you hear me?"

"Loud and clear. A word of warning, if I may. When the outer door opens it will be total blackness outside.

You best hold onto me, or you will get completely disoriented."

Mia sighed. "It's sols like this when I wonder why I do this job."

An orange beacon pulsed inside the airlock to signify decompression, and the outer door began to open. Dense clouds of dust seeped in as the gap widened, billowing all around them and blocking out the pulsing beacon. The dust continued swirling around, filling the airlock until Mia could see absolutely nothing. She could barely make out her own hand in front of her.

"Holy crap, it's impossible to see anything." She felt Gizmo's metal hand grab her and gently tug her forward. She tentatively followed, one cautious step at a time.

"Do not fear. I can see the terrain perfectly, and there is a flat concrete apron around most of this sector. Just take it slow." Gizmo guided her out. "We should move farther down along the edge of the buildings just in case they send a detail out here to check."

Mia followed as Gizmo moved off slowly. She hadn't been out on the surface since the start of the dust storm, and so had no idea just how visually debilitating it was. That, along with the fact that she was attempting this at night, meant that she could see nothing but the reflective glare from her helmet instruments on the inside of her visor. Beyond that, it was total blackness. The ground underfoot was firm, as Gizmo had said, so her speed increased a little as she grew in confidence.

Mia had been moving steadily for a few minutes

when she sensed a sudden increase in illumination, followed almost immediately by a slight ground tremor. She spun around to locate the source and saw a giant ball of gaseous flame spew out from the airlock side of Lloyd's warehouse.

"Holy shit, they've blown up the place." Another ball of flame spat out as some store of flammable gas exploded. It was short-lived, as all the oxygen had now been expunged from the interior.

"Oh my god, everyone in there must be dead. No one could survive that."

"I calculate the probability of survival at 4.7%," said Gizmo, as the robot scanned the facility. "We best take cover. We will have shrapnel raining down on us at any moment. It may damage your EVA suit."

Mia found herself entombed in darkness again as Gizmo guided her into the lee of a structural wall, hoping to mitigate against the worst of the debris shower. As she waited for the droid to give the all clear, Mia began to consider her options.

Lloyd and his crew were probably dead, either from the explosion or the dramatic decompression. It signified a serious escalation in the levels that Montecristo were willing to go to to keep a lid on whatever it was they didn't want people to know about. When they took out Agent Dan Frazer, it was made to look like an accident, so they had spent some time planning that. But this was different. A full-frontal assault, no attempt to hide it—they must have felt they had become so powerful that they would face no repercussions for such blatant action.

So, what now? she thought.

"The debris has passed, Mia," the little robot's voice echoed in Mia's helmet. "Fortunately, I have a complete schematic of Syrtis downloaded and have assessed all entrance points into the city. There are a number that we could utilize to gain entry back into the city with a low chance of being spotted. The closest is approximately 1.3 kilometers northeast of our current location."

Mia remained silent for a moment as she considered this option. "Then what, Gizmo? What do we do once we're back inside? The MLOD here aren't going to help us. Lloyd was probably right about them being in the pocket of Montecristo Industries. If we go back to the MLOD, then we would need some strong evidence, something they can't ignore. Otherwise, the only other option is to hightail it back to Jezero City empty-handed."

"I cannot answer these questions, as it is an operational decision for you to make."

"How far is it to the Leighton waystation from here?"

"Approximately 3.2 kilometers."

Mia checked her EVA suit resources. "This suit has around four hours of air. Would it be possible to walk there and back in that time?"

"Under normal conditions it would take less than an hour to walk that distance. But these are obviously not normal conditions. I can navigate there, but you will be effectively blind. From my limited observation of your current abilities, I calculate a four-hour round trip, assuming you want to return to a city entrance."

"Four hours. That's cutting it a bit tight."

"Indeed."

Mia thought about this. It was possible, but only just. There would be no room for dealing with the unexpected. That being said, from what Lloyd had told her, Leighton was more like a small town, so that meant the possibility of getting the EVA suit resupplied. "Gizmo, how much do you know of the layout of Leighton?"

"Fortunately, I had the good sense to acquire the schematics from Lloyd before his untimely demise."

"Okay, let's do it. Everything we've learned so far leads to that place. So, we go and find out what we can. Hopefully it's something we can use to force an investigation into Montecristo and their methods."

"Very well, then. Stay close—this will not be easy."

11

LEIGHTON WAYSTATION

After a half hour of walking and stumbling in the total darkness, Mia became very claustrophobic. She felt entombed in her EVA suit, like some reanimated, twenty-first-century Egyptian mummy.

"Gizmo?"

"Yes, Mia?" the droid's voice crackled in her helmet comm.

"Do you think it's safe enough now to use our lights?"

They had planned to keep them switched off and try to make it to Leighton without using them, just in case they might be spotted. But now Mia was getting desperate for something—anything—to focus her eyes on, even if it was just a swirling cloud of dust.

"I cannot say for sure if it is safe. Our best option is to remain stealthy and minimize our visual footprint."

"Nobody is going to see shit out here. I can't even see

my own hand. I need something to focus on and not have to keep holding onto you."

"Very well, but it is not going to help much." With that, the droid switched on a powerful light on its upper body.

Mia also switched on her own helmet lights, and for the first time in over a half hour she could see something other than total nothingness. But Gizmo was right: even with all this illumination, it failed to penetrate the thick dust farther than a meter. Yet it was enough for Mia to let go of the droid and be able to follow it simply by its illumination.

They continued like this for another half hour. The terrain had become rougher, but they were making faster progress now. Soon, Mia began to sense a dim glow emanating from deep within the dust storm.

"I think I see something."

"Yes, the outskirts of Leighton. It is not far now. I am taking us to an airlock on the eastern side. If the schematics that Lloyd Allen provided are accurate, then this should lead us into a little-used sector. Hopefully we can gain access without being spotted."

"How much farther?"

"Ten minutes. I suggest we switch off our lights and travel the rest of the way in stealth mode."

Mia switched hers off and the darkness closed in around her. She reached out to place a hand on Gizmo in case she lost it in the gloom. They journeyed in this manner for a while. All the time, the glow emanating from the dense fog grew in intensity. Soon, Mia began to define several light sources, presumably coming from the outlying buildings of the old waystation.

Gizmo took them past these structures and they traveled along the boundary for a few more minutes, until finally a small, squat dome materialized out of the fog. They had reached the airlock.

It had an old-fashioned industrial look to it, all rivets and interlocking bars. It looked more like the door to a bank vault than an airlock.

"Are you sure this is it, Gizmo?"

"Are you seriously asking me that question?" the droid replied, a little irritated.

It moved over to an illuminated keypad and examined it for a second or two before starting to disassemble it. A few moments later, a green overhead light illuminated and the door swung open.

"Easy-peasy," said Gizmo.

They entered, closing the outer door behind them. The airlock began to pressurize again. "You know," said Gizmo, "it is very inconvenient, all this pressure equalization needed for humans to move from inside to outside."

"Not as inconvenient as dying."

"True, but I do appreciate the fact that, as a robot, I do not need air, nor one atmosphere of pressure to continue to function."

"Well, I'm very happy for you, Gizmo. Just don't suddenly forget that I need it, okay?"

"Of course not. It was simply an observation."

A green light flashed, and the inner airlock door opened into a dimly lit, deserted corridor. To Mia, even this extremely low-level illumination was like being bathed in brilliant sunshine, and it took a moment for her eyes to adjust. Already, Gizmo had exited the airlock and was scanning the area. "Just as I had concluded —deserted."

Mia popped open her visor, and her nostrils were assailed by a foul, acrid stink. "Oh my god, what's that smell?"

"My sensors detect elevated levels of ammonia in the composition of the air. I suspect it is a byproduct of the bioreactors operating in this sector."

"Can you show me a map of our location? We need to figure out what our next move is. Hopefully it's somewhere other than here."

They moved back inside the airlock for a moment, and Gizmo projected a 3D schematic of the area into the space in front of it. "This sector is primarily industrial: water treatment, gas manufacturing, industrial chemicals."

"That smell is probably why they have it located out here and not in the city." Mia pointed to another sector on the 3D map. "What's this area?"

"Warehousing and logistics, then workshops and maintenance," said Gizmo. "And farther along is the main population center and transport hub, with all the accommodations located at the very farthest point from here."

"Warehousing?" Mia thought for a moment. "That would seem like a likely place to store components."

"If I may make a suggestion."

"By all means, but make it quick."

"Most of this sector is controlled by Montecristo. If I can get access to a terminal then I may be able to hack into their systems and get some insight into their operations here."

Mia poked a finger at the droid. "Brilliant. That's exactly the reason I reanimated you and brought you along on this investigation."

"Well then, I shall not let you down. Just give me a moment to do a deeper analysis of the electrical systems in this schematic and find a network interface."

Mia detached her suit gloves, followed by her helmet, into which she stashed the gloves, finally clipping it onto a shoulder strap designed for this specific purpose. With that out of the way, she was free to use both hands. She reached into a cargo pocket on her right thigh, withdrew her plasma pistol, and prepped it for operation.

"If my analysis is correct, and it always is, there should be a network node at the far end of this corridor. It should be unmanned, but that I cannot be certain of."

"Okay, let's get it done. Lead the way."

THEY MOVED out of the airlock and down along the dim corridor. Mia had her weapon in hand, set on stun, and was ready to shoot anyone who got in her way. The walls on both sides were punctuated with doors every five meters or so, each with a four-digit alphanumeric identifier stamped on it in large, blocky lettering.

"This is it. A546." Gizmo stopped and examined the door's keypad. Mia took up a position beside it, her back to the wall. She held the pistol up, ready for action.

"I would suggest not using that weapon inside this room, Mia."

"Why not?"

"High-intensity plasma and delicate electronics do not work well together."

"Well, too bad. Because if there's someone in there, then we have a problem. So, I'll tell you what, Gizmo: I'll try not to miss."

"Very well, it is your call." The droid had already disassembled the keypad. "Are you ready?"

"As I'll ever be."

The door clicked and opened silently inward. The room was bigger than Mia had imagined, around six meters square, and stacked floor to ceiling with racks of servers, their lights blinking and flickering like a thousand multicolored stars. Sitting at a small workbench, a stunned technician had just enough time to register his shock before Mia blasted him square in the chest with a bolt from her plasma pistol. He fell to the floor, his body encased in a flickering mesh of electrical fuzz.

Mia turned to the droid. "Happy?"

"Excellent shooting. True to your word, you did not miss."

"Okay, now it's your turn. Let's see what you can dig up." Mia moved back to shut the door as Gizmo began to interface with the Montecristo network. A 3D rendering of the entire Leighton facility blossomed to life on a small holo-table protruding from a stack of servers, and several other monitors sprang to life with fast-scrolling data. Gizmo twitched a little as it analyzed the incoming data stream.

The holo-table flickered through a multitude of three-dimensional views at a speed far beyond Mia's ability to process.

"Interesting."

"What is?"

"I am aggregating warehouse access data, looking for deviations and anomalies."

"What does that mean?"

"All activity around the storage and warehouse facilities follows a similar pattern as goods are moved in and out. I am looking for facilities where this deviates, and I think I have found one." Gizmo swiveled its head at the 3D rendering, which froze on a static view, and pointed. "It seems to be centered on that location."

Mia moved closer, examining the rendering as it slowly zoomed in on a specific sector close to the transport hub, with several small, secure storage facilities all in a neat row. They were all tagged with an alphanumeric code.

"I have analyzed all activity in these sectors over the last month to establish a base pattern. Then I looked for deviations on this—outliers, so to speak. Things that would highlight activity that does not follow the norm. Of the sectors that deviate, this one is the most inconsistent."

"So, you think they might be storing these components here?" Mia pointed to the location on the schematic.

"Yes. Also, they have conveniently identified it as such." A label popped up on the image, reading *Electronic Component Storage.*

"Well that's very nice of them. So where is it, and how do we get there?"

"Tricky. It is located adjacent to the transport hub, which means we will need to find a route through the busiest sector in this facility."

"Meaning there's a high likelihood we'll be spotted."

"Correct."

Mia glanced down at the unconscious tech lying on the floor and considered relieving him of his uniform. He was much taller and broader than her, so it wouldn't fit very well, but she might get away with it. However, it would mean ditching her EVA suit, something Mia was loath to do. Not having a suit would lessen her escape options, but on the other hand, it would make her much more conspicuous.

"I have plotted a route that should minimize our interaction with the general populace," said Gizmo as the 3D schematic over the holo-table zoomed out, with a line indicating the route overlaid on the map.

Mia studied the route. "That's going to take us directly through the main transport artery of this facility, Gizmo."

"Correct. But there is no other alternative—we must pass through it."

Mia consider this for a moment, then glanced down at the tech and back to Gizmo. "Can you get a video feed of that area?"

"Yes, that should be possible." The monitors flickered monetarily, and the scrolling data stream was replaced with live camera feeds.

The intersection that they needed to cross was busy with people, droids, and autonomous carts transporting goods. Mia even spotted a few G2 units. This was good; it meant that Gizmo would not be noticed. As for the people, they all wore face masks and an eclectic assortment of work-wear. She might get away with keeping the EVA suit—all she needed was a face mask. If they were quick, they could be through without anyone noticing.

"They have a lot of droids. It looks like there is no shortage of spare parts in this facility." Mia then turned to the unconscious tech and removed his face mask. He was still out cold, but for how long? "What do we do with this guy?"

"Judging by his size and weight, he will be incapacitated for approximately one hour. But that is not a very accurate assessment."

"Well, I don't want to tie him up just in case this is a room no one else comes into for weeks at a time."

Gizmo moved back to the terminal. "Last access in

here was...ten sols ago."

"How long will it take for us to get to the storage sector and back to the airlock?"

"Assuming you find what you want without a prolonged search, then I estimate thirty-five minutes."

"Okay, we leave him as he is and take the risk." Mia covered her mouth and nose with the face mask and moved to the door. "Lead the way, Gizmo."

IT DIDN'T TAKE LONG to start meeting traffic. A small autonomous truck came trundling around a corner, followed by another. Then three workers passed them, but paid no attention to Mia or her G2 unit. By the time they arrived at the main artery, they had been passed by several groups, but again, no one seemed to pay any attention to them. Mia kept her head down, her mask up, and focused on following Gizmo.

It took them a further fifteen minutes to reach the secure storage sector—a long, wide, deserted corridor with several heavy metal doors along one side. Although there was no one in this sector, Mia assumed there were cameras everywhere. They would need to get in and out as quick as possible. Hopefully they could get back out through the same airlock they had entered by, and then walk back to Syrtis, where Mia would contact MLOD, present them with the evidence, and push for a full investigation.

"This is it," said Gizmo as it came to a halt before a

sturdy vault door. It moved over to the keypad control and started to disassemble it.

Mia stood with her back to the wall, checking the entrance to the corridor in case anyone showed up. The door thumped and hummed as the locking bolts retracted, and it gently swung open. They stepped in.

The room was sizable, with a high ceiling of possibly five or more meters. It was also crammed with packing crates, the type used for interplanetary transport—meaning these goods had come from either Earth or possibly Ceres, out in the asteroid belt.

Mia rubbed a thin film of dust from the side of one of the crates to reveal a stenciled alphanumeric code and the Montecristo Industries logo. She then found the catches and flipped open the lid. Inside, buried in a sea of packing foam, were hundreds of components.

"Looks like you were right, Gizmo."

"I am always right, Mia."

She picked out a small component, vacuum-sealed in a translucent plastic package. "If I'm not mistaken, this looks very similar to the one Lloyd showed me."

"Yes, it is a logic controller, hardened for high-radiation environments."

"I think these are from emergency aid shipments. The packaging is stamped *Intervention*."

"That is possible. But we do not have access to the shipping manifest, so we cannot be certain."

"Gizmo, go check some of the other crates."

"Mia, I need to stress the urgency of the situation. We

must get back to the airlock before the tech in the network room wakes up. We do not have much time."

"Just do it quickly then, Gizmo."

BETWEEN THEM THEY opened several more crates, all containing components with the same label stamped on the protective wrappers.

"These are all from emergency supplies." Mia looked at the droid. "Do you realize what this means?"

"They are not circumventing the embargo."

"No, they're not. They're simply siphoning them off from inbound inventory. Basically stealing. These should be destined for critical life-support systems. Holy shit, this is big. We've got to get this out."

"Then I suggest we make haste, as time is not on our side."

Mia began grabbing bunches of components and shoving them into pockets on her EVA suit. "Okay, that should be enough. Time to get out of here."

The lights in the storage area all suddenly came on, and two Montecristo security personnel appeared in the doorway, weapons pointed directly at Mia and Gizmo.

"Hold it right there." They started to advance.

"Shit. Gizmo, there's no way out."

"Indeed. The probability of a positive outcome to this scenario is zero."

"You don't say." Mia thought about going for her plasma weapon, but it was buried in the bottom of a pocket under a pile of components. She considered her options.

She could simply run at them, as the EVA suit would offer her some protection from the PEP weapons. And Gizmo could handle a few shots, too.

"Gizmo, when I give you the word, we run at them, try and barge our way out into the corridor, and lock them in."

"If you say so, but I estimate the probability of—"

"I know, I get it... Zero."

"I was going to suggest that I go ahead of you, as I will be able to absorb more of the weapons fire than you."

"Okay, good plan."

"Stay where you are. Hands in the air." There were only two meters between them now.

"Now," Mia shouted.

Gizmo raced forward. Two shots hit the robot before it reached the guards, but it made little difference to its momentum. It barreled through, knocking one down. The other stepped aside as Mia raced after the droid.

They were nearing the door, and Mia thought they would make it when she felt a plasma blast rip through her lower back. Her muscles went into spasm as searing pain rippled through every nerve in her body. Her legs ceased to function, and she collapsed face down on the floor. Her vision blurred, and her brain struggled to stay conscious. She was aware of Gizmo trying to drag her out the door as it took a barrage of direct plasma fire. But she drifted out of consciousness, and her world went dark.

12

BLACK-COAT MAN

Somewhere deep within Mia's unconscious brain, synapses fired to test her physical state. It established that her pain response had lessened to a point that would be bearable, and, other than a lot of bruising and surface trauma, she was mostly intact. So, it decided it was time to bring her back to consciousness.

She awoke slowly, aware of cold at first, then light, and finally that she was tied to a chair in an empty, nondescript room. But she was still alive. That was something, at least.

As she came to, Mia tested the bonds that restrained her, pulling and twisting this way and that, but they held fast. She then moved on to examining the room. The light was dim, and the room big enough that she could not see its outer walls. On the floor she could see scraps of wrapping strewn around, as well as loose and torn straps. She was in a storage room, probably not far from where they were apprehended.

Gizmo, she thought, and looked around again, trying to find some evidence of the droid in the room. But there was none. "Shit," she shouted out in frustration, and tried again to break her bonds, tugging and twisting with all her strength. But it was no good. She wasn't getting out of this on her own.

She heard shuffling sounds coming from deep within the gloom. "Gizmo?" Mia strained her ears to hear. The shuffling sounds continued, getting closer. Finally, out from the darkness stepped two men. One wore a long, black coat that wafted around his legs as he moved. The other wore the black uniform of Montecristo security. She could not make out their faces, as they were encased in complex face masks.

"So, you're finally conscious." The voice had a low, hissing quality to it. Mia could not see who spoke, but assumed it was the black-coat man.

"Screw you. Where's my droid?"

"Your droid is spare parts, or soon will be. As for you, let's have a little talk."

Mia clenched her fist and strained the bonds holding her down as black-coat man came closer, stopping less than a meter from her.

"Do you know who I am? There will be hell to pay for incarcerating an MLOD agent." She tried to put some venom in her voice.

He folded his arms and considered her, tilting his

head slightly to one side. "We know who you are, Major Mia Sorelli, so let's not pretend to be all indignant and self-righteous. You're all alone here, with just me and my friend." He gestured at the armed security guard. "So, care to tell me who else knows you're here?"

"MLOD HQ back in Syrtis, for one. And they are going to be so pissed with you when they find out—" Mia didn't get time to finish her sentence, as she was whacked across the face with the back of a gloved hand.

"I'm going to ask you again, except this time let's make it a little bit more interesting." He reached inside his long, black coat and pulled out a sleek-looking plasma pistol, then took a moment adjusting something on its side. "Amazing technology, when you think about it, these PEP weapons." He held it up to the light and admired it. "Such delicate control over the levels of pain that can be administered. You know, back in the day, they used to use ballistic weapons. Small bits of metal exploded out from a barrel. Very crude, no finesse." He held the weapon up again. "But these, on the other hand, are the very pinnacle of pain-delivery technology." He turned it sideways in his hand, brought it closer to her so she could see it, and pointed at a small, thumb-operated dial. "You see here, this setting is *certain death*." He then turned the dial all the way down and showed it to her again. "But this setting here won't kill you, just inflict excruciating pain. Although, I've always wanted to know what would happen if someone took a direct shot to the brain." He stepped back a little and held the weapon to the side of her head. "Only one way to find out, I suppose. So, one more time—who knows you're here?"

The barrel pressed hard against her temple, and Mia heard the faint squeal of the weapon charging. She may survive a single shot, but her brain would probably be fried.

"Dan Frazer."

There was a momentary pause as the man in the black coat tried to make sense of this answer. "The MLOD agent? He's dead." He leaned in a little closer to Mia. "That's what happens to people who get too nosey and go poking around where they shouldn't." He gave a laugh and looked across at his colleague.

So, there it is, thought Mia. *Mystery solved. This guy or his associates must have killed him.*

"Why?" she ventured.

"I'm asking the questions here." He pressed the gun's muzzle harder against her temple and held it there for a moment before suddenly taking it away and reaching for his earpiece comms. "What?"

There was a pause as he listened to some message.

"No, I'm fucking busy..." He turned his back to Mia and continued listening to the message. Whoever was communicating with him was not taking no for an answer.

"Okay, give me five." He sighed as he turned to face Mia again. He aimed the weapon at her forehead, and Mia considered that this might be it. Game over. She gritted her teeth and held his stare for what seemed like an eternity, until he suddenly shoved the weapon back inside his long black coat. He pointed a finger at her. "We're not done here yet, you and I."

Mia breathed again as he turned to his colleague and gestured to him. "Let's go." They walked out the way they came, back into the darkness.

Mia's heart raced, her body pumped adrenaline, her breath came in gasps. She had been given a reprieve, nothing more. She was still trapped with no way out. Again, she tugged and twisted the bonds that held her, but this time it was with a demonic fury that she did not realize she possessed. But it was futile; she was only doing herself harm. Eventually, she gave up and tried to examine the chair more closely to see if there were any structural flaws she could utilize.

It was strong and heavy, but with a certain amount of effort she found that she could move it, but only slightly. Yet it was the only thing within her control; she had no other options. But move to where? The storage room was sizable, too big to see its full dimensions in the dim light. To explore it would take more effort than she had in her. Maybe she could find something on the floor that she could use to cut her bonds. This might be possible. The floor was littered with the detritus of packing cases. It might be possible for some scrap of metal to be lying around. She started moving, one tiny increment at a time.

It took her a few minutes and a considerable amount of effort just to rotate her position in the space a full 180 degrees. She wanted to get a view of what was behind her, in the hope that there may be something lying on the floor that she could use. But as she scanned the area, she saw nothing useful. She rested for a moment, gathering her strength for the next effort, when she heard the shuffling return.

Goddammit, she thought, *they're back.* Mia figured she would've had more time, but it was not to be. The game was finally up. Yet the sounds were different—lighter, softer, and more numerous. Mia's brain was trying to work out what, or who, might be making them when a masked faced came around from behind her, holding a long, serrated knife. She stiffened in response. The figure reached up and removed his night vision goggles and mask.

Mia looked at him in shock. "Lloyd?"

He put a finger to his lips.

"How the..." she whispered.

"Long story. Let me get you out of here first." He proceeded to cut her bonds.

She rubbed her wrists to get some feeling back and stood up. She was very shaky and unstable, and rested a hand on Lloyd's shoulder. Two more people came into view, both well-armed. One signaled to Lloyd to hurry up.

How is he here? she thought. *How did he survive the explosion at the warehouse?* All these questions swelled in her head as she began moving across the storage space. But they would have to wait. The fact was he was here with some of his crew, and she was getting out. Getting answers to her questions could wait.

"Gizmo," she croaked. "I need to find Gizmo."

"It's over by the entrance." Lloyd pointed ahead. "But it's scrap metal now. The power cell was removed—it ain't going anywhere."

As they moved through the dim space, Mia could see it wasn't completely empty. Stacks of packing crates appeared from the gloom. This led them into a workshop area when Gizmo stood, silent and mute, wires sprouting from its innards.

"Gizmo, what have they done to you?" She raced over to it as fast as her battered body would allow.

"Come on, leave it. We gotta go," one of the others called over to her.

"I'm not leaving without it."

"Are you totally crazy? It's just a droid. You can always get another one."

"It may just be a droid to you, but to me it's a friend, and I'm not leaving it."

"Shit, I knew this was a bad idea, Lloyd. Her brain is fried."

"Come, we'll carry it between us." Lloyd rushed over to where Mia stood and ran his eye over the droid. "These old G2 units are heavy bastards."

The others reluctantly complied, and between the four of them they hauled the droid out of the storage area and into a dimly lit corridor.

As they moved, Mia noticed that Lloyd was listening to messages coming in on his earpiece comms. Somebody was coordinating their escape, possibly someone on the inside—someone looking at the security feeds and directing them when to move and when to stop.

They made their way without incident to an airlock, and it was only then that Mia realized none of them were wearing EVA suits. She had woken up in the storage area without hers. Presumably they had taken it off her when they found all the components she had risked so much to obtain. The evidence was now gone, unless Lloyd and his crew had managed to acquire some, which meant her mission here was all for nothing. Without the components as evidence there was little she could do to kick-start any formal investigation.

The outer door opened, and they all piled in. It was a tight squeeze with the droid, but they managed it. Mia had that momentary feeling of panic that people who live a pressurized life on an alien planet get when stepping into an airlock without an EVA suit. *Will there be pressure on the far side?* The others all looked calm, so she assumed they had come here with transport. The outer door opened, revealing a cramped rover interior. They piled in, closed the door, and the machine disengaged, moving off slowly.

After a few moments, Lloyd and the crew began to relax a little. Weapons were put aside and face masks removed. It was only then that Mia could see it was Anka and Milo who had accompanied Lloyd on this rescue mission.

Mia rubbed her face and glanced over at Lloyd. "Okay, so how the hell did you guys survive that explosion?"

"Ah...it was us that blew the place up. Took out a lot of Montecristo security in the process." A wide grin grew across Lloyd's face.

Mia shook her head. "I thought you were all dead. I thought myself and Gizmo were on our own."

"We knew this sol would come, knew they could attack us," said Lloyd. "We had an escape plan in place."

"So how did you find me? How did you know I was in the Leighton waystation?"

"Your EVA suit. I put a tracker on it." He gave her another broad grin. "Hope you don't mind."

"Not from where I'm sitting. All I can say is thank you. I was sure I was a dead woman. I couldn't see a way out."

Lloyd nodded. "Happy to be of service."

Mia looked around the rover's interior. "I thought you didn't have a working rover?"

"We don't. We stole this one from Montecristo." He winked.

The rover began to slow, and Mia realized that something must be up, as Lloyd stood up and moved into the cockpit where Marcus was at the controls. Anka and Milo were picking up their weapons, and the mood changed to one of high alert. The rover finally stopped just as Lloyd stuck his head back into the cabin. "Panic over. Marcus just got lost."

"I'm not lost—I know exactly where we are. I'm just taking the scenic route is all," Marcus shouted back from the cockpit. "You try finding your way in this shit."

Anka and Milo put the weapons down again and

relaxed. Lloyd returned to the cabin and sat down opposite Mia.

She leaned in, elbows on her knees, hands clasped, and started telling him what she'd found. "We located the unit they were using to store the components. At least, Gizmo did." She looked over at the forlorn robot for a moment. "But it was only when I entered that I realized the extent of the crime. Crates and crates of components, stacked floor to ceiling. We're talking thousands of components."

"Are you serious?" Lloyd looked genuinely shocked.

"That's not all. You guys have been working on the assumption that they were somehow breaking the embargo, finding a way to bring in direct shipments from Earth."

"You're saying they're not?" said Anka.

"All the components we found were from intervention stock," said Mia. "They're siphoning off the supplies coming in as emergency aid."

"Holy shit." Anka was stunned. "This is serious. The people have to know about this. There'll be even more riots once this gets out."

Mia shook her head. "Who's going to believe us? We have no hard evidence, just my word against Montecristo. That's not going to get us anywhere."

"Did you grab any of them when you were in there?" said Milo in a soft, almost apologetic voice.

"Sure I did. I stuffed a load into my EVA suit. But then we got caught, and, well...you know the rest."

"So, we're back to square one," said Anka.

"Not necessarily," said Lloyd. He was looking over at Gizmo. "Dragging that droid out of there might have been a good idea after all." He looked back at Mia. "The droid would have recorded it. If we could get it operational again, or even tap into its datastack, we might get something we could use."

"That would be something," said Mia. "But it's probably not enough."

"Well, we may not even get that." Lloyd shook his head. "Things have developed fast since you've been gone. The situation in Syrtis is deteriorating rapidly."

"Why?" said Mia. "What's going on?"

"Montecristo have sent a large cohort into the maintenance sector. They're trying to take it over—by force. Our people have taken up arms to defend themselves, so there are pitched battles going on all over the sector."

"What about the MLOD?" said Mia. "Are they not trying to stop this?"

"Ha...you forget that the MLOD has contracted Montecristo to deal with security on the streets," said Anka. "Their hands are tied, so they're turning a blind eye to everything that's going on."

"I don't believe this. What about the MLOD in Jezero?" Mia continued.

"What about them? They don't care about us." Lloyd waved a hand in the air.

Mia sat back and pointed a finger at Lloyd. "You get

me a comms link when we get back, and I'll get you some law and order. You have my word on that."

"Even if you can persuade Jezero to intervene and send people, it's going to take a while." Lloyd was not convinced. "It may be too late by then."

"You just get me that comms link."

"Okay, but I have to warn you...we may be heading straight into a shitstorm."

13

VANCE BAPTISTE

Vance Baptiste gave a long, satisfied sigh as he relaxed in his oversized jacuzzi, letting the water jets work their magic, massaging his ample body. To his annoyance, he noticed that his fingernails still had a noticeable layer of dirt, which had accumulated after his short visit to the planet's surface to meet with Chief Becker and that troublesome Major Sorelli from Jezero. He sighed again, this time with a hint of resignation, and went to work cleaning them. He found that even the briefest of visits to the surface always resulted in him needing a thorough and comprehensive decontamination routine.

Fortunately, the meeting had been short, and he had wasted no time in returning to his private orbital, preferring the comfortable one-G environment and the clear, pure air to the filth and poverty of the planet's surface.

How anyone chose to live there was beyond his understanding.

Back when he agreed to undertake the job of Director of Advocacy for Montecristo Industries—a contract with such ludicrous remuneration and side benefits that he simply couldn't turn it down—he did so on the proviso that he would not have to spend any more time on Mars than was humanly possible. So far, this had worked out reasonably well; mostly he ran all operations from the comfort of his luxury space station, where he could enjoy all the pleasures of opulent living without the need to physically expose himself to the squalor of the masses.

Montecristo needed him because they had a problem. For all their power and influence on Mars, the one prize that had eluded them was control of the governing council. Yet they were close, very close. They had spent well, buying off those who could be influenced by money, funding those who were sympathetic to their mercantile ambitions, and eliminating roadblocks where needed. But one sector stood in their way, a sector where no amount of corporate spend had any impact on its citizens —and without them, Montecristo Industries would always be one district short of complete and absolute control of the governing council of Mars.

To break this deadlock and inject some fresh thinking into the problem, they sought out the talents of one Vance Baptiste, a man who had achieved startling results for the Valdivian Corporation on Ceres, not to mention several others on Earth. His job was to do what the entire board of Montecristo had so far failed to do, and that was to subjugate the citizens of the maintenance sector to their dominion. And, as good fortune would have it, the worst dust storm ever encountered on Mars had just kicked off, leading to Montecristo—and by extension, Baptiste—having primary control over all shipments of vital spare parts, the one thing that everybody wanted. It was better than money, it was power. And Baptiste relished every moment when he could wield this power. That was, until the fly that was Major Mia Sorelli had decided to embed itself firmly in the ointment of his ambition.

His ruminations were disturbed by an incoming comms alert flashing on his ocular implant. It was Joshua T. Becker, chief of police in Syrtis. He considered ignoring it, as it would just be an irritation to his current relaxed state. But then again, he did find toying with the chief to be quite entertaining. He gestured with an outstretched hand to establish a comms connection, and a holographic projection of the chief materialized in mid-air around a meter in front of Baptiste.

"Ahh, Chief. Forgive me if I don't reciprocate the visual feed, as I'm somewhat indisposed at present."

"She's still alive. We've just received reports of a stolen rover heading for the maintenance sector with Sorelli and a number of other radicals on board."

"Hmmm...she is proving to be resilient."

"We're not exactly sure where she is," Becker continued, "but there are not too many places where she can hide."

"We need to find her, for both our sakes. She has managed to get farther than Agent Frazer did by gaining entry into the storage facilities in Leighton, and then managed to escape with the help of her recently acquired band of radicals. Fortunately, she came away empty-handed. But we need to nip this in the bud, Becker."

"You have the all-clear from the MLOD to do what you have to do," said Becker. "Just try not to blow anything up this time. That entire sector is a hotbed of reactionaries and subversives, all itching for a fight."

"Well, maybe it's time we did something about that. Major Sorelli may have presented us with an opportunity to deal with this problem once and for all."

"Don't get ahead of yourself, Baptiste. There's still a lot of resistance to Montecristo's involvement with the MLOD as a security partner, and that last attempt by your security personnel on Lloyd Allen's warehouse angered a lot of people. The rumor mill has also been dialed up; lots of talk that Agent Frazer was eliminated by Montecristo."

"Just talk and nothing more, I assure you, Chief. Our only interest in all this is how we can help maintain law and order. It's in both our interests, and it's good for business."

"So you keep saying. But there are other rumors. It's beginning to leak out that Montecristo are stockpiling vital components, keeping them out of circulation, exacerbating the failure of vital systems."

"The people who are spreading this sort of poison need to be dealt with. This does nobody any good."

"Just letting you know."

"I appreciate that, Chief. But just remember who's helping the MLOD hold the line here. Without our continued assistance, there would be civil breakdown, utter chaos. So, we both need to work together on this. You keep everyone out of that sector. We'll do the mop up and get these radicals brought to justice."

"Try not to blow anything up this time."

"Listen, Becker. If we need to blow something up, then so be it, and you're just going to have to live with that. So have your people coordinate with my people and let's get this done." He terminated the comms.

By now, Vance Baptiste had spent too long in the jacuzzi, and his primary concern was that his body would start to resemble a dehydrated tomato. He stepped out and wrapped a thick, warm dressing gown around himself.

This Sorelli officer was becoming a serious problem, and Chief Joshua T. Becker was getting spooked. True, she came with a pedigree that stood her apart from the normal foot soldiers of the MLOD. Therefore, it was highly unlikely that she would just go off and die the same way Dan Frazer did. Nevertheless, she needed to be gotten rid of, along with the other rabble.

Fortunately, she had come away empty-handed from

her incursion into the Leighton waystation, but she had picked up a cohort of very troublesome friends along the way. Lloyd Allen had been a thorn in Montecristo's side for a long time, single-handedly preventing them from taking control of that sector of Syrtis—something that Vance Baptiste's paymasters were not happy about. Not happy at all. And their botched attempt to apprehend Sorelli at his warehouse had failed in spectacular fashion.

But now it seemed that he had a golden opportunity to put it all to right. He now had the authority to do whatever it took to flush them out and take control of the last important sector in the city. Then... Well, he was getting ahead of himself. Best not get too cocky. There was a lot of work to do.

He gestured with an outstretched hand and opened a comms channel to Montecristo's head of security, Orban Dent. *Time to get this show on the road,* he thought. A thin smile cracked across his face.

A HIGHLY DETAILED 3D schematic of the entire maintenance sector of Syrtis hovered above the large, central holo-table in the main operations room of the orbital space station. A now fully dressed Vance Baptiste studied it carefully. Hovering above a secondary holo-table was an almost life-sized avatar of Orban Dent, Montecristo's head of security and their man on the ground. He was currently located in the corporation's HQ back down on the planet's surface. Together, they were coordinating their efforts to find Sorelli and her associates.

Knowing that the MLOD agent and her ragtag crew of reactionaries had returned from the Leighton waystation was one thing, but actually locating them in the maze of walkways, buildings, and facilities in the sector was considerably more difficult. They could be anywhere.

Their rover had been tracked inbound as far as the number two navigation beacon, one of a long line of beacons placed on the route to facilitate surface travel in the dense dust storm. After that, they had lost track of it, yet it was assumed to be somewhere in that sector. If it were anywhere else, they probably would have found it by now.

But this sector had always had a strong, defiantly independent streak. It didn't help that a good deal of its denizens were technically well versed, so had set about undermining all attempts by the Mars Law and Order Department, and its security contractor Montecristo, to monitor the comings and goings in this area.

But the authorities still had their ways. It was more difficult, but not impossible, to get a digital picture of the activities within. The numerous technicians arrayed around the operations room had now been diverted from all other activities to focus solely on this one single task: find Mia Sorelli.

Vance Baptiste looked up from the schematic and directed a question to Orban. "Well?"

Baptiste suspected that Orban still felt responsible for letting Sorelli escape from Leighton. He'd had her locked down good and tight, yet he had neglected to consider that her newfound buddies might come looking for her. Yet he shouldn't be too hard on himself; they must have had inside help. How else would they know where to find her and how to evade their security? Still, he needed to make it right. He needed to find her.

Baptiste also suspected that Orban did not whole-heartedly approve of his methods, preferring instead to fall back on the old ways that had proven ineffective in advancing the corporation's objectives. When it came to one on one, Orban Dent had few equals, but he had no stomach for full-frontal mass assault and the invariable body count it entailed.

"We're still correlating data streams," Orban's avatar replied. "Nothing definitive as yet. However, we have intercepted an encrypted tight-beam comms signal emanating from within the sector to Jezero City. Its digital signature suggests it could be the work of Lloyd Allen. It has his fingerprints all over it."

"So they're in there somewhere." Baptiste rubbed his chin and glanced back at the holo-table. "Can you decrypt it?"

"Working on it. We're confident, but it will take time."

"How long?"

"I understand it to be imminent."

"Good. We need to find these bastards and eliminate them. They've been a thorn in our side for too long. I say we just go in there with overwhelming force and take these scumbags out once and for all."

"I suggest we be more patient and strategic. Your last foray in there didn't work out too well, did it?"

Baptiste felt a twinge of anger at Orban's criticism of his methods, but he resisted the temptation to lash out at him, preferring instead to try to bring him around to his way of thinking. He needed him on board, so he would just have to play the game.

"Okay, we do it your way. We take our time, find out exactly where they are, and then strike. Just don't forget that we've been presented with a golden opportunity to finally bring this sector under our influence. Once that is achieved, we will then have effective control of Syrtis, which in turn will give us control of the council—and that means control of Mars itself." He stabbed a finger at the 3D schematic hovering above the holo-table. "This sector holds the key. It is the final piece of the jigsaw that Montecristo Industries has been working toward for a very long time."

"Understood," said the avatar.

"Also, Chief Becker has given tacit approval for an armed intervention, and we need to keep him and MLOD on our side in all of this. Although I suspect that the chief is having doubts. His resolve is wavering in the face of the brutal reality of armed subjugation of this band of radicals. But if we are to ultimately reach our goal of complete control of Mars, then this is our opportunity. We are on the cusp of greatness, Orban, so let's not screw it up."

Orban's avatar cupped a hand over his right ear. "I think we have it. Comms connection has been decrypted." A red marker started flashing on the 3D schematic. "Coming from that location."

"Excellent," said Baptiste, clasping his hands together. "Do we know what was in the message?"

"Putting it on the table now." With that, a grainy head-and-shoulders hologram of Mia Sorelli materialized, along with an even more grainy rendering of council member Poe Tarkin, Director of Planetary Security.

"Tarkin?" Baptiste cocked an eyebrow. "This should be interesting."

But the feed was of poor quality. The image flickered and degraded into fuzz. The audio was slightly better, but they could only make out snatches of the conversation.

Baptiste shook his head. "Why is this so bad?"

"It's the nature of this type of comms. The highly charged atmosphere created by the dust storm makes it problematic."

"Problematic? This is shit! What the hell are they saying? Can we clean it up?"

"Working on it."

Baptiste concentrated and tried to make some sense

of the fragments he could pick up. The transmission began to stabilize as the techs worked their magic on it, and soon he began to make out some of the conversation. Major Sorelli was explaining what she had found at the Leighton waystation, and a momentary pang of fear surfaced from deep within Baptiste. But he needn't have worried, as Tarkin proceeded to berate Sorelli for effectively going rogue.

"We sent you there on a simple mission. Now you've turned it into a revolutionary crusade. The council are saying you've gone all Patty Hearst."

"Who?"

"A historical figure who was co-opted by a bunch of crazies."

"This is serious, Poe. Montecristo are siphoning off essential supplies, undermining our very survival. How many people have died in systems failures that could have been prevented if the new components were available?"

"Look, Mia. I'm not doubting what you're saying. Montecristo have been growing ever more powerful since the MLOD in Syrtis decided to hand over their security to them. I don't trust them, and neither do a lot of us, but—and here's the problem—you don't have any evidence, Mia. I can't convince anyone here to take action without cold, hard evidence."

"Just go to Leighton and take a look."

"We can't. Not without good reason, and you haven't given us any."

Baptiste glanced at Orban. "That's interesting," he said

before returning his focus to the communication. Poe Tarkin was still talking.

"You need to get out of there. Your continued presence is just going to give them an excuse to take over that sector. You're just playing into their hands."

"You can stop them, Poe. Just give the order to Chief Becker to hold off until I get the evidence we need."

"I'll try, Mia. That much I can do. But I think you overesti-mate the power the council here has over the administration in Syrtis. The chief is in the same position as we are, if not worse, in trying to keep a lid on complete social breakdown. The MLOD need Montecristo. Without their people, they would have a hard time keeping control."

"Not if the thousands of stockpiled components were released. Things could be fixed. Things would improve."

The transmission began to fragment until it finally ceased all together.

Baptiste turned to his head of security. "Do we have a location yet?"

"Yes. It should be on your holo-table now." The holo-graphic schematic of the maintenance sector reappeared, this time with a blinking location marker.

"Well get in there now, before Chief Becker has a change of heart. Once we start the operation, he can do nothing to stop it.

Baptiste thought he detected a slight hesitation in his head of security before he finally replied. "Right away, sir."

"As soon as Sorelli and that Allen radical have been

dealt with, then move onto the second phase. Full occupation, okay?"

"Very well. First contingent is now on its way."

"Excellent." Baptiste returned to studying the map of the maintenance sector as a thin smile rippled across his face.

14

REVOLUTION

I t wasn't so much that Mia didn't know where she was or where she was going. It was more that she didn't know what she was doing, nor was she sure of what everyone else was doing, for that matter. Events were moving ahead of her, and she was struggling to catch up.

The conversation with Poe Tarkin had proven fruitless. Her faith in the directors of the Mars Law and Order Department to do the right thing were failing, even before she embarked on this mission. But now, after talking to Poe, it was shattered. He seemed more concerned about the consequences of sticking his neck out than with *doing the right thing*. They were hanging her out to swing, something Mia had a lot of experience in, and not a place she wanted to be—not now, not ever.

Nonetheless, she could see that the optics of her situation did not look good. Unbeknownst to her, Lloyd Allen was far from the benign, slightly eccentric, good-hearted tech nerd that she had initially supposed. In reality he was knee—deep in fomenting a pushback against the all-pervasive influence of the Montecristo Corporation, and by extension the MLOD. And, he and his associates were not opposed to using violence to further their aims. In the romantic worldview, they were rebels fighting for the people. However, in the cold political reality of the Council of Mars and the institutions that governed the planet, they were simply vigilantes.

Maybe Poe was right: she should find a way to get out —and fast, before the shit hit the fan—and leave Lloyd and his band of freedom fighters to their high-minded delusions.

Part of her felt that she had been used, a useful pawn in their corporate fight. She had the wherewithal to get the evidence they needed to turn the populace against the enemy, so what if she got burned in the process? Was that what had happened to Agent Frazer? Had he also been a willing pawn, set up by Lloyd to do the dirty work, even though his life was at stake?

Her mission was to find out what had happened to Frazer, not embark on a crusade to take down some corporation, even if they were screwing people over. She was just doing her job: to seek the truth, to seek justice. And look where that had taken her. She had pulled at the thread, and now the whole goddamn thing was unraveling.

. . .

BUT THEN AGAIN, they had come back for her, risked their own lives to get her out, even though they knew she had effectively failed in her mission to acquire hard evidence of Montecristo's duplicity. So, there was that. And there was no doubt in her mind that the extent of the deceit that had been uncovered needed redress. The lie needed to be exposed, people needed to understand what was happening, and they needed to get angry—very angry. The only problem: most people in the sector preferred to do what the MLOD were doing.

Look the other way.

THEY HAD TRAVELED BACK to Syrtis, avoiding the last few navigation beacons and feeling their way through the impenetrable dust storm like some nocturnal animal, mapping their surrounding by sense of smell alone. How it was done was a mystery to Mia, but to her relief they arrived in a vehicle maintenance facility, another ware-house not unlike the one she and Gizmo had left when they began their long walk to the Leighton waystation.

Who owned this place? No one said. But Mia got the impression it was yet another one of Lloyd's *assets*. It had a semi-derelict feel to it, with an acrid smell typical of a facility that had gone without atmosphere for some time. It was virtually empty except for the scavenged hulk of a long-forgotten rover. Yet from seemingly out of nowhere, in the space of a few minutes, the crew produced an impressive array of weapons, surveillance equipment, and even a fresh pot of coffee.

"Plan B," was all Lloyd said to her with a wink as he busied himself getting the equipment operational. Milo was dispatched out into the sector to inform "those who needed to be informed" of what had been found in the Leighton waystation, and to "expect trouble." Marcus disappeared, only to return a short time later with yet another small handcart full of weapons and an announcement that "all preparations had been made." And all this time, Gizmo lay in the hold of the rover, a broken, disemboweled mess.

Yet Lloyd had been true to his word, and through some feat of technical magic had established a comms link with MLOD in Jezero, enabling Mia to seek help from Poe Tarkin. Now, though, it was all for naught. No help was forthcoming. And to make matters worse, when Anka and Milo returned, it was with news that "those who needed to be informed" were not happy that they were being dragged into an armed confrontation with Montecristo security simply on Lloyd's word that they were depriving the citizens of life-saving supplies.

"Ungrateful bastards." Marcus stomped the floor and kicked the side of an old metal crate, sending it flying across the floor.

"So, what was the mood out there?" asked Lloyd. He looked up from the bewildering array of data feeds he had been studying on the rudimentary holo-table that had been set up.

Marcus shrugged. "If shit goes down, they'll help us, as always. But not with any sort of conviction. There are plenty who see us as just causing trouble."

Lloyd shook his head. "I can't say I blame them. It's hard enough just to survive these sols, let alone take on the ever-growing arrogance of Montecristo."

"We need get the word out to the people," said Anka. "Not just in this sector, but all over Syrtis. We need the people to really see what's going on. We need to get it out on the grid, let everybody hear what these guys have been doing to us."

"Nobody is going to give a shit," said Marcus. "That's just pointless propaganda. Let's face it, we've been forced to play our hand too early, and we've failed. All we've succeeded in doing is to embolden Montecristo. Now it's only a matter of time before they come for us."

"What about Gizmo?" Mia sat on an old crate, nursing her bruised and battered body. "It should have recorded everything up until its power cell was pulled. If we could access the datastack and broadcast it, that might move people to take action."

"Nice idea, but not so simple as it sounds. We don't have the spare parts to get it operational again." Lloyd shook his head.

"We don't need it fully operational, we just need to access the data," offered Mia.

"Again, not so simple. For one, that droid operates on older, more esoteric protocols than most stuff we have now. Secondly, everything in there will be encrypted.

Even if we could access the data, it would take a considerable amount of time to make sense of it. And time is one thing we don't have."

"What about trying again?" said Anka. "Going back to the Leighton waystation and getting what we need?"

"Not without Gizmo." Mia shook her head. "It was the only reason I could get in, get past the security, and find where they were storing the components. It's not possible without it, especially now that they know. The place will be locked down tight."

Anka slumped down on a crate beside Mia. "So, what do we do?"

"Make no mistake, that bastard Baptiste is smelling opportunity, and he's coming for us. So, I say we stand and fight. And there are others in the sector who will stand by us—we can be sure of that." Lloyd was not giving up.

"Yeah, screw them." Marcus raised his plasma weapon in the air.

Mia sat there and wondered where all this was heading. They were all gunning for a showdown, and now was as good a time as any, as far as Lloyd and his crew were concerned. But was this just gung-ho naiveté, or did they really stand a chance of turning the tables on Montecristo?

There was already a flurry of activity as the crew got to work. Marcus and Lloyd gathered around the holo-table and started studying the layout of the sector. Anka sat down at a comms desk and started contacting other groups, warning them of a possible attack.

Mia sat for a moment watching all this activity, feeling somewhat at a loss as to where she fit into all this proto-revolutionary fervor, when Lloyd came over and sat down on a crate opposite.

"You don't have to be part of this, Mia. You can take the rover and get out of here. Follow the edge of the city until you pass this sector. You can re-enter Syrtis somewhere well away from here. Try to make your way to MLOD HQ."

"And then what? Frazer was an MLOD agent and it didn't work out so well for him. Do you think I'll be any different?"

Lloyd looked vaguely apologetic. "But you're from Jezero. Baptiste won't try anything once you're back out in the open."

"Maybe, but I still have to deal with the fallout from 'going rogue.' There would be plenty of opportunity in that situation for something unfortunate to happen to me."

They sat in silence for a moment before Mia rose and moved over to the small handcart full of weapons. She picked one up and examined it. "You know, Lloyd, sometimes the only way out...is to go in deeper." She flicked a switch on the weapon; it made a high-pitched squeal as it charged. "I can't go forward and I can't go back, so it looks like I'll just have to go through."

15

RIOT DROID

Mia didn't do waiting very well. Without something to keep her mind and body occupied she would find herself receding into her thoughts. This was dangerous territory for her, as the longer it went on, the darker her mood got. So it was, after several hours of hanging around in the maintenance hangar, watching the others make preparations for their defense against Montecristo's security, she felt a growing sense of fatalism well up inside her.

In the face of the worst dust storm ever recorded on Mars, slowly etching humanity off the planet, what were we doing? she thought. *Using it as an opportunity to screw each other over. And for what? Power? Control? Money? Or maybe all of the above?*

What was the point of even fighting, of trying to do the right thing? She wasn't even sure what the right thing was anymore. Doubling down and throwing her lot in with Lloyd and his band of revolutionaries?

She needed to do something, anything to get her mind away from its ceaseless descent into darkness.

During this time, more people arrived. Several small groups came and discussed options and strategies before leaving again. Some remained, eager to throw their firepower in behind Lloyd and the others. It was as she watched all these comings and goings that she began to realize the extent—and depth—of feeling amongst the citizens of this sector. They saw it as a fight for survival. It wasn't just the endless dust storm that they were fighting, but also those who would use it as a tool in their lust for power—at least, that was how they saw it. Mia realized how isolated Jezero was from these people. Back there, in the shiny corridors of power and the manicured tourist parks, no matter how bad things were, it was nothing compared to this.

For the people of this sector, their greatest fear was that they just didn't matter. They didn't trust Montecristo's slow takeover of power, seeing them as duplicitous and motivated solely by the advancement of the corporation they represented. They feared that as soon Montecristo gained control, the people of this sector would be expendable, nothing more than an inconvenient roadblock to the mercantile ambitions of the corporation. As for Jezero, the MLOD, and the institutions of law and order, they saw them as the willing levers of power that the corporation sought to assimilate and ultimately undermine. In short, Montecristo didn't give a shit about anybody but themselves.

Mia understood now the root of their animosity toward both her and Gizmo that first time she entered the sector and started snooping around. What she also didn't know back then was how deep this rage went. Looking around her now, she could see that it was all coming to a head. Perhaps she played some part in that—perhaps her actions were the catalyst. But it was coming, with or without her. This sol was inevitable.

"Incoming," one of the techs shouted out, jolting Mia out of her reverie. "Two groups... Looks like they have at least six riot droids with them."

The tech, along with several others, were sitting at a cluster of data screens and holographic displays. It had been all set up over the last few hours as the group made their preparations for the forthcoming confrontation. On the holo-table, a sizable 3D schematic of the entire sector blossomed out. Mia could see red dots illuminating the locations of two separate intrusions, moving slowly along a wide thoroughfare that bisected the sector. They were coming in from either end.

Lloyd came over and studied the schematic. "Okay, tell everyone to get ready... And can we get video on this?"

On screen several feeds materialized, displaying a cohort of twenty or so heavily armed security personnel in each group. Ahead of them, several riot droids formed a line across the route as they moved.

Then, at around three hundred meters from their

position, both groups stopped moving. Mia watched in tense silence with the rest of the crew, waiting for the next move. But nothing happened.

"What are they doing?" said Anka. "They're just standing there, doing nothing."

"Boss," one of the techs called over to Lloyd. "Looks like we have a request for comms coming in."

"From which group?"

"It's not any of us, Boss. It looks like it's from the MLOD."

"What the hell do they want?" said Marcus. "And how did they get our channel?"

"What do you want me to do, Boss?"

Lloyd thought for a moment. "Put it on speaker."

"This is Chief Joshua T. Becker of the Mars Law and Order Department. Who am I speaking to?"

Lloyd exchanged a few glances with the rest of the group before replying. "Lloyd Allen. What do you want?"

"I imagine that asking that you all put down your weapons and give up this pointless exercise would be a complete waste of time, so I'm not going to bother."

"You would be correct. So, like I said, what do you want?"

"Is the MLOD agent Mia Sorelli there with you?"

All eyes turned to Mia, and there was a moment's silence.

"I'm here," Mia finally replied.

"Poe Tarkin, Director of Planetary Security, has pleaded your case with us here in Syrtis. And it is with deference to

him and the council in Jezero that I am willing to offer you a way out of this."

Again, all eyes turned to Mia.

"Go on."

"We have agreed to give you the opportunity to leave here and turn yourself in. You don't have to die here with the rest of these scum."

There was a momentary pause as Mia considered her response. "And what happens then?"

"You will of course be put on trial for your part in this...charade. But at least you have the chance to get out of this alive. It's the best we can offer, and you need to thank Director Tarkin for arguing for this, since you...eh, were a high-ranking MLOD officer."

"I see. Tell me, Becker, do you know why I was sent here, to Syrtis?"

"I don't have time for this, and frankly, I don't care. I just need an answer."

"To investigate the death of Agent Dan Frazer. And do you know what I found?"

"Save it for your trial, Agent Sorelli."

"I found that the MLOD here in Syrtis are a bunch of spineless cowards."

"Right, I've had enough of this. It seems you've spent too long in the swamp of radicals. You've become brainwashed into their paranoid reality. You've exactly three seconds to decide."

"Tell Director Tarkin thanks, but no thanks. I'd rather take my chances here."

"Your loss. Goodbye."

The comms went silent, and for a moment all eyes again looked at Mia. This time it was with a new sense of admiration.

"They're on the move," the tech shouted out. "Droids in the vanguard."

Lloyd glanced at the video feed. "Okay, it's time to hit them."

The tech sent the command out to units farther up the street.

Suddenly, the wide doors of two industrial units flew open and the carcasses of old rovers were shoved out, forming a barricade. The same action was also being performed simultaneously at the other end of the street. Fighters massed in behind these and unleashed a barrage of fire at the oncoming riot droids.

The screen was filled with the incandescent blue rage of multiple plasma blasts dancing around the droids' hardened outer shells. One staggered, then righted itself before two more direct hits finished it off and it crumpled to the ground.

The security guards, who were content until this point to let the droids do all the work, now started returning fire. Mia could see one rebel down, lying motionless, while a second was been dragged away by a comrade.

The barricade was now taking a sustained hammering as the attackers tried to provide cover for one of the riot droids to move in closer and start to shift the rover carcasses.

Lloyd turned to Marcus. "Time to get down there and lend a hand. We don't want them breaking through."

"Too right." Marcus was studying the feeds intently.

"Take everyone you can."

"On it."

With that he signaled for the fighters who had assembled in the warehouse to follow him. Mia checked her weapon.

"Not you, Mia," said Lloyd.

"Why not? I can fight better that most of your people, from what I've seen so far."

Lloyd cast her a wry eye. "I don't doubt that, not for a minute. That's why I want you here, in case things get hairy." He smiled. "I reckon you would be pretty handy in a tight spot."

Mia put her weapon down and moved over to get a better view of the feed, now that most of the fighters had cleared out of the hangar.

Already, the droid had reached the rover barricade and was starting to shift it. Its metal hands clamped onto the frame, ripping at it as it tried to find purchase. Two more droids moved slowly in behind. A fourth, farther back, seemed to be out of action. Behind that, the security detail advanced, keeping low and tight against the side walls of the street.

The battle at the other end of the sector was faring better. Only two droids were in use there, and Mia got the sense that Montecristo's strategy was to keep them just

busy enough to commit fighters and stop them from rein-
forcing the main assault.

Lloyd was getting anxious. Mia could sense it in him
—the intense stare, the twitchy body movements. At this
rate, she might get her wish, as the fight looked like it was
coming to her.

There was a sudden, intense burst of fire from behind
the barricade as Marcus's people moved in to reinforce
the position. The droids halted, and the attackers began
to move back.

A side door opened down the street a little way in
front of the makeshift barricade. Mia could just make out
a small object being thrown out. She assumed it was a
grenade of some kind. It arced through the air and
landed on the back of the droid that was trying to disassemble the barricade. It stuck onto its casing like a
magnet. For a moment nothing happened, and the droid,
realizing something had attached itself to its back, tried
to remove it. But before it could, it simply crumpled on
the floor.

This seemed to be the signal for a renewed barrage of
fire from the fighters. The two remaining droids started to
retreat; the security detail behind them did likewise.
After they had retreated to around a hundred meters
from the barricade, the fighting stopped. Mia could see
that the contingent at the other end of the street had also
retreated.

There were whoops of joy, and some fighters even

clambered up on the carcass of the rover to shout taunts at the attackers.

"They backed off," said Mia in a surprised tone.

"For the moment." Lloyd was more circumspect. "They'll be back, and soon. That was just the opening salvo."

"What was that weapon that took the droid down?"

"Ahh, a localized EMP—electro-magnetic pulse weapon —of my own design. Highly effective against these droids." Mia could see he was impressed with himself. "Takes out the control circuitry, leaves the power source intact."

Mia turned back to the video feed of the celebratory rebels, but her attention was focused on the fallen riot droids. Two were down, now just crumpled heaps. There was something reminiscent in their design and construction that reminded her of Gizmo, and G2 units in general.

"Those droids." She pointed to the image on the monitor. "What type of power cell do they use?"

Lloyd glanced at her and then back at the monitor. He remained silent for a moment, long enough for Mia to think he may not have heard her. He turned around and gave her a considered look. "It might be possible. It might." He stroked his chin for a moment.

"They use an old-school, low-energy nuclear reactor —a LENR. Very similar to your own droid, Gizmo."

Mia moved in a bit closed and studied the fallen robots. "Are they too damaged, or would the power source still work?"

"That one there should be okay." He pointed to the droid nearest the barricade.

"Is it worth trying to get it?"

"Hmm." He started stroking his chin again. "Possible. But to what end?"

"If we can get Gizmo working, even just enough to get access to all its recorded data from Leighton, then we could broadcast it, people would see and hear the truth, and we could change the tide of opinion, start a goddamn revolution."

"I think Chief Becker might be right about you. All this talk of revolution sounds like you've been spending too much time with the wrong people." He gave her a smile.

Mia shrugged. "Just tell me you can do it. Can you get Gizmo working?"

Lloyd glanced back at the monitor. "Hmm...maybe. We need to drag that thing back in here and hope it doesn't wake up in the process. Then I can see if it's possible."

"Get me comms with Marcus." Lloyd called over to one of the techs, then turned back to Mia. "Just so you know, even if we get this thing in here, there are still no guarantees. I'm going to need time, and that is in short supply."

"I understand, Lloyd. But we've got to try."

16

JEZERO

The first skirmish had not gone the way Vance Baptiste had hoped. True, it was just an initial encounter, a probe to test the resources and resolve of the rebels. But he had clearly underestimated what it would take to dislodge them from their warren. Yet it was not something that couldn't be overcome by simply throwing more at it. That had been his initial strategy—go in hard and heavy. But it was Chief Joshua T. Becker's desire to keep it under the radar as much as possible, coupled with Orban's desire to minimize collateral damage, that persuaded him to take the softly-softly approach. Now, though, all gloves would be off. He needed to resolve this situation and quick, because word had gotten out and other sectors were getting more agitated.

Orban's avatar brought a 3D map of Syrtis up on the holo-table in the operations room on board Baptiste's orbital. "We have several outbreaks of violence across the city. Nothing major, just minor skirmishes and altercations." He pointed to several sectors in turn. "It looks like word has gotten out about the fight going on in the maintenance sector, and some folks are using it as an excuse to cause trouble."

Baptiste grunted. "All the more reason to get this situation under control as fast as possible. So, no more dicking around, Orban. We go in hard and heavy. Get it done."

"Easier said than done. The problem with these minor incidents is that they're sucking in our personnel. We need people on the ground to deal with them."

"Well, you best get them put to bed. I want all resources focused on that rebel warehouse."

Orban pursed his lips as he studied the 3D map. "I get the feeling that the rebels might be behind some of these skirmishes—as a way of keeping us busy."

"Don't be stupid. They're rabble, they don't possess that level of sophistication."

"Maybe so." The avatar turned to face Baptiste. "There is another option, if we want more resources."

Baptiste raised a hand. "Don't say MLOD. I don't want to hear it."

"Why not?"

"Because you know as well as I do that we're under contract to deal with all this shit. If we have to go ask for their help, then there will be no end of bureaucratic hoops to jump through."

But Orban was being insistent. "The fact remains that if we want to go in hard and heavy, then we're going to need more resources. That means taking them from elsewhere. I estimate we could bring in twenty or so, but for any more, we need to start getting the MLOD to do some of the riot control."

"Riot?" Baptiste stiffened. "You didn't mention a riot going on."

"Here, in this sector." A new marker blinked on the 3D map. "It's not a riot yet, but it has the potential."

Baptiste glanced at the 3D map, then to one of the video feeds. A large crowd of around fifty or so were milling around waving placards, ranting about air quality.

Baptiste sighed. "I think you might be right, Orban. This smacks of distraction." He knew then that he had no other option. He needed to give Chief Becker a call.

"No way. I'm already taking a lot of heat by letting you start a small war in the maintenance sector." Joshua T. Becker was almost shouting over the comms link. "And Tarkin over in Jezero is not happy about their agent being stuck in the middle of it all. It seems they've had a change of heart. Now they want her out."

"What the..." Baptiste's frustration was rising. "She had her chance. What's more, you and I can't afford to have her walking around alive."

"Listen, Tarkin has taken an ear-bashing from the

council in Jezero on this. Apparently she's some sort of national hero, so they don't want her dead."

"Well, it's too late for that now."

"Also, we have another potential problem."

"Oh, for fuck's sake, what?"

"The MLOD in Jezero have decided that the situation here is becoming too volatile. I think they're afraid of contagion. So they've taken the unprecedented step of loading up a shuttle with security personnel and are sending them here."

"Ha, ha... They're risking a shuttle flight for this? They must be pissed."

"This is no laughing matter, Vance. This is a serious escalation. You need to get your Montecristo people on the council in Jezero to get this stopped now, before they take off."

"Hmm... Well, having extra officers here could work to our advantage." Baptiste paused for a beat while he considered this development, then returned to the comms link. "Becker, here's what you do. Let them take up crowd suppression. That lets you off the hook and allows us more resources to deal with Lloyd and that Sorelli bitch. You'll just have to swallow your pride. In fact, I suggest you invite them in, say they are needed urgently."

"I don't like it. These Jezero types are not like us, all full of their own self-importance. They could do more harm than good."

"When could they get here?" Baptiste was not interested in listening to Chief Becker's protests.

"I don't believe this. You're not actually serious."

"Becker." Baptiste's voice was sharp. "You need to realize that it's not your call. When you took the opportunity for the high-life that we here at Montecristo offered, it came with a price, and that price is full, one-hundred-percent compliance. So you do as I say, or we'll find someone else in the MLOD who will."

There was a momentary silence as Chief Joshua T. Becker took this in.

"Look, Joshua." Baptiste's voice was more conciliatory now. "We have an opportunity here to get everything we want. So let's just get it done. By tomorrow morning, you and me will be having a celebratory drink and laughing about it."

There was a long intake of breath from Becker. "Okay, but just get it done fast. I don't know how long I can keep control of my end."

"How long does it take to get from Jezero by shuttle?"

"An hour and twenty minutes, normally. In this dust storm, who knows. Nobody flies anymore unless it's critical."

"Well, what's critical is that you start getting your people on the streets so we can do what we have to do. You'll just have to hold the line until backup from Jezero arrives."

There was another long sigh from Becker. "Okay, but they're not going to like it down in HQ."

"They don't have to like it, they just have to do it."

BY THE TIME Vance Baptiste had finished his conversation with the chief and returned to the operations room, there had been some new developments, some of which made no sense to either him or Orban. Apparently, the besieged rebels had just broken out and moved their barricade farther up the street, taking some losses in the process. The reason for this bizarre act was so that they could drag the carcass of a dead droid back into the warehouse.

"When did this happen?" Baptiste's eyes were fixed on the video feed of the street.

"Just now. They've only been back inside a few minutes."

Baptiste pursed his lips. "Why would they do that? It doesn't make sense."

"It must make sense to them."

"Are they trying to fix it, get it working?"

"Unlikely. It would be extremely difficult to do that, and it would take a considerable amount of time. Time they don't have."

"So what, then?"

"Maybe they think they can salvage its weapons systems?"

"Maybe. But whatever it is they're up to, they must think it's worth taking some losses for."

A tech call came over from a console in the operations room. "Sir, I have just received confirmation that the MLOD are deploying resources to all the trouble spots."

"About time. As soon as they're in position, I want all our people and resources moved to the maintenance sector. That includes you and me, Orban. We're going manage these operations directly on the ground."

"You're coming down to the surface?" Orban's avatar flickered momentarily.

"Damn right I am. This is too important an operation. That, and I would like to be there when we finally crush them."

"I'll make the necessary preparations."

"Meet me at the old shuttle port. I'll land there; it should be safe enough away from the city. And have the mobile operations unit up and running. We're gonna need it."

"Very well. Let's hope we have enough spare resources to quell this uprising," said Orban.

"We will. And remember, we always have the ultimate weapon if they prove to be too well dug-in."

Orban's face morphed into a genuine look of shock. "You're not seriously considering using that?"

"If I have to, I will. These people need to crushed, not just in body, but in spirit, too."

17

PROPAGANDA

It was evident to Mia that Lloyd was a brilliant engineer, but as a revolutionary leader, he was struggling. His modus operandi had always been defense. Protection of his personal space, along with that of the wider maintenance sector community. All this stemmed from the loss of his robotics business to the corporate forces of Montecristo. So fundamentally, he was not some visionary radical—far from it. He was pragmatic and practical. His support came from former workers and their extended networks that had an enormous amount of respect for him. That, and the fact that he had the residual wealth and expertise to acquire and maintain considerable resources.

But everything they had done so far was as a reaction to Montecristo and their ever-expanding power base. They had done nothing more than give the corporation an excuse to enter the maintenance sector and wipe out all opposition. Defense, in this instance, would not win the war. It was a fight to the death, and there would only be one winner. Therefore, if they were to prevail, then they would need to expose Montecristo.

Lloyd, of course, knew this, but his failing was that he had not planned for it. Clever strategies for evasion, the provision of safe houses, and the ability to organize protests to divert resources were all defensive, not offensive. In the Revolutionary 101 guidebook, taking control of state media was at the top of the list. The ability to supplant the propaganda of the current power with that of your own was the key to turning the tide.

Lloyd's plan only went as far as digging up some dirt on Montecristo, something that he could use against them. But Mia realized that the only way out of this current situation was to take them down completely, and the best way to do that was to expose them. But the evidence would need to be absolutely irrefutable, as the propaganda machine of Montecristo Industries would seek to undermine its validity. Simply broadcasting the data that Gizmo had stored may not be enough, but it would be a good start, and would certainly buy them more time, maybe even force a stalemate.

Mia reacted suddenly to a ruckus emanating from the warehouse entrance. She looked over to see Marcus and three others dragging in the immobile riot droid. It was much bigger than she had envisioned from the video feeds. The scars of battle were evident all across its tough outer casing; deep gouges and burns seemed to cover every part of its humanoid form.

It twitched.

"Stand back," someone shouted. "It's still alive."

Everyone jumped back, weapons aimed and ready. There was a tense moment as they waited for some other action from it. But nothing more happened.

"Has it done that before?" Lloyd directed his question to Marcus.

"Twice before, while we were dragging it in here. Scared the shit out of us the first time."

"Good, good." Lloyd stroked his chin.

"I hope to hell this is worth it. We had three people go down getting this...thing."

Lloyd's face morphed into one of deep concern. "How bad?"

"Bad enough. One's critical." Marcus gave the engineer a hard look. "Just make it worth it, okay?"

Lloyd nodded and got to work.

TECHS DRAGGED over diagnostic equipment as Lloyd clambered atop the dead machine and started delving into its innards. Several others stood by, weapons ready, just in case. Mia made her way to the rover and, with the help of a few others, they dragged the disemboweled Gizmo over to where Lloyd and the techs were working.

Perhaps she was being overly optimistic. After all, there was no guarantee this was going to work. But she had to believe it was possible. Part of her didn't care about the data so much—it was more to see Gizmo back in action. In truth, she missed the droid. It was the one entity that she could trust. She could always rely on it to cover her back, and it was her friend.

The riot droid twitched again, sending the group into high alert. Lloyd was now sitting at a terminal screen, intently studying a stream of scrolling code. The droid twitched even more, then its arm started to move.

"Lloyd, are you doing that?" Mia, along with several others, took a few steps back and aimed their plasma weapons at the machine as it began to reanimate.

"It's moving, Lloyd." Mia's voice held a note of concern. "What do we do?"

"Gimme a second." Lloyd waved a hand in the air while continuing to look at the monitor.

The droid began to move its head, then its other arm. It was trying to stand up.

"Lloyd!" One of the others was getting panicked. "Either you kill this thing or we do."

"Just wait, wait. I'm trying to override it."

They all took another step back as the machine rose up to full height and its sensor array began to scan the group who now circled it, weapons at the ready. A section of its right shoulder cracked open, and the muzzle of a plasma cannon appeared.

"Lloyd, you've got one second to get control or we take it down," Mia shouted out.

With that, the droid collapsed in a heap on the floor of the warehouse.

"Got it," Lloyd shouted over from the terminal.

"Are you sure?" Mia was taking no chances, dancing around the inert heap, weapon in hand, ready to fire.

"Yes, yes, it's not getting up again." Lloyd stood up from the terminal and came over. "Sorry, I didn't realize it had a secondary backup system. Once I rerouted the power supply it came back online. But it's okay now, it's totally offline. And the good news is that the power cell is still operational."

Mia relaxed and lowered her weapon. "So, you'll be able to get Gizmo working again?"

Lloyd stroked his lower lip with the back of his thumb. "We'll see. No guarantees, though."

But before Mia could reply, a tech shouted over from the holo-table, "You'd better take a look at this." He was studying a hologram of the city that radiated out across the surface of the holo-table.

"What is it?" said Lloyd as he, Mia, and a few others stood around the map.

"We have reports of MLOD activity. Looks like they're moving into sectors where there's trouble. They're relieving Montecristo's security. See here."

Several video feeds materialized above the 3D map. Mia could see uniformed MLOD officers milling around several other sectors of the city.

"We don't have much time," said Mia. "Montecristo are

preparing for another assault. You need to get Gizmo working as soon as humanly possible."

The tech cupped a hand over his ear, then looked over at Mia. "I'm getting a report that a shuttle from Jezero City just landed, with thirty or more MLOD officers on board."

"What, here in Syrtis?" said Mia.

"Yes, that's what I'm hearing."

Mia stood silent for a moment, thinking. "Actually...this could be good," she finally said. "Shuttle flights are rare these days, so if they are sending that many, they must think the situation on the ground here is critical."

"Yeah, but whose side are they on? That's what I'd like to know," said one of the fighters who had returned to the warehouse after the battle for the street.

"Eh, I don't think it's ours." Anka pointed at the broadcast feed.

Images of MLOD officers moving out across the walkways and plazas of Syrtis flickered on the screen. They were taking up positions in all the trouble spots. A running commentary ran along the bottom of the feed, outlining the fact that forces from Jezero were being deployed as a back-up for the local officers. Together they were confident about quelling the insurgence currently active in the maintenance sector.

"We've got to counter all this...propaganda they're spewing out." Mia was getting increasingly frustrated at not being able to do anything about it.

But before anyone could answer, the tech brought up

a new feed, this time from within the sector. "We may have a problem."

The view was down along the main thoroughfare, directly outside the warehouse building. In the foreground, the wreckage of the barricades could be clearly seen; along with the detritus of the last battle, crumpled machines and debris were strewn everywhere. The tech adjusted the camera and zoomed in to focus far off at the very end of the thoroughfare. There, shrouded in a hazy mist, a formidable machine advanced. It moved on eight legs in a slow, graceful ballet, its head a turret from which a long, pointed snout emerged. Mia, along with the others in the group, watched in silence as the machine advanced, skewering parked ground cars and storage containers along either side of the thoroughfare with each downward thrust of its many appendages.

"Holy crap, what the hell is that thing?" said Mia.

"Spider tank," said Lloyd a little casually, as if he had seen it all before. And perhaps he had. "But it's not a tank in the military sense. They just call them that. They're used for asteroid mining. See the way it's engineered, like a spider? That makes it good for traversing very rough terrain."

"Does it have weapons?" said Mia.

"Not officially. However, it has a ballistic cannon used to blast craters on the asteroid's surface so that it can sniff the resultant dust cloud for trace elements using an onboard spectrometer."

"Sound like a goddamn tank to me," said another of

the fighters. "I assume that pointy bit on the turret is the cannon?"

"Correct." Lloyd seemed fascinated with the machine.

"Holy shit, ballistic weapons?" Marcus began to stomp around. "That thing could blow a hole in the sector dome. That would be catastrophic. We're talking mass extinction of the population."

The rest of them watched as the machine advanced, a line of black-clad security personnel moving in behind it. Mia stopped counting at thirty, and there were many more than that.

"We need to get up high to have a chance at taking that thing down. If we're on street level it will blow us to pieces." Marcus had stopped his pacing and began to focus on the problem. "We take positions up along the rooftops. They won't risk firing that thing at us in case they hit the dome."

"Let's hope you're right," said Lloyd.

Marcus moved to the comms desk and started barking orders to the units out on the street, then gathered up his crew and headed out to battle.

AFTER SOME ARGUMENT, Mia reluctantly agreed to remain behind with Lloyd and one other tech. He reasoned that if they could get Gizmo active again and get the data, then Mia needed to be the one making the broadcast, not him, since he had been labeled a reactionary and a radical. His name was toxic.

It had to be Mia.

But she was damned if she was just going to sit around like a spare part. So, she took over monitoring comms, freeing the tech to help Lloyd disassemble the riot droid.

She paced up and down, watching the spider tank advance as the rebels took up positions along the rooftop. And all the while, in the background, the broadcast media pumped out rolling coverage of the MLOD deployment in the city.

It had all finally come down to this. What should have been a battle to get the truth out, to reveal the perfidy of Montecristo, had now become simply a battle for survival. *And what of Jezero?* she thought. *What was their role in all of this?* Mia pondered these questions as the moment of confrontation drew ever closer. She had known from day one that the MLOD here in Syrtis were not on her side. But Jezero? These were her people, her tribe. She could not believe that they would desert her now, in her hour of need. That was why it had to be her face on the broadcast; she could appeal directly to them to do the right thing. She had to believe that they would see through the propaganda and subterfuge.

Then again, to risk a shuttle flight and send so many must be putting the social stability of Jezero under enormous pressure. There would be those who would hate her for forcing them into this position, risking the stability of Jezero to stop the crisis in Syrtis from destroying them all—a crisis partly of her making.

The ground trembled, and the 3D image on the holo-table rippled in concert with the vibration.

"Shit, what was that?" She spun around and looked at Lloyd.

"Ballistics," Lloyd replied without looking up from the belly of the riot droid he and the tech had disemboweled. "They've started."

Mia glanced back at the video feed from the street. Lloyd was right: the spider tank wasn't firing upward, it was simply taking the buildings out from street level. She could see a gaping hole in the row of structures, filled now with a tangled mess of twisted, crumpled metal. A hail of plasma fire rained down on the tank from the rooftops on either side, to no apparent effect.

More plasma fire lanced out from behind the makeshift barricade just as another shell from the tank exploded a few meters in from it. The fighters ran for cover as the tank moved in for the next shot that would surely take it out completely.

"LLOYD, unless you can get Gizmo working in the next few minutes, we're gonna be out of time. That tank is mowing down everything in its path."

Lloyd lifted out a section of the droid's innards. "That's not enough time. It'll take at least another thirty to get this power cell hooked up, and I still don't know if it's going to work."

"Shit, we need to buy more time somehow. What about those EMP devices—would those stop it?"

Lloyd shook his head. "No more left. We just had one."

"Then we're done. Plasma weapons aren't going to stop that thing."

Lloyd pursed his lips. "Wait a minute. I've an idea." He ran back to the carcass of the riot droid. The tech was already running diagnostics on some the components that they had extracted earlier. Lloyd clambered on top of the dead droid and started to hack at it.

"What's the idea?" A note of desperation had entered Mia's voice.

"Fight fire with fire," said the engineer, freeing a short, stubby cylinder from the carcass. "Plasma cannon power supply." He held it up to show her. "This has potentially an enormous amount of stored energy. Short-circuit it and all that energy is released in a high-intensity reaction."

"A bomb?"

"Sort of, depending on how much energy is left in it. It won't explode as such, but it will burn at a temperature high enough to melt the casing on that machine. If it burns long enough, it will start to drip inside and destroy the tank from the inside."

Mia left the desk and came over. "Can you get it to detonate?"

"Working on it." He attached the unit to a screen terminal and started perusing lines of code.

The tech was looking over Lloyd's shoulder at the

screen. "You could expose the core. Then a high-intensity plasma blast could be enough to melt the insulator, and boom."

Lloyd looked at the tech for a beat. "You're a goddamn genius. That could work."

They then set about dismantling the unit.

"I'll do it," said Mia, after a few minutes.

Lloyd gave her a concerned look. "No, let Marcus take care of it. You don't have to go."

"We don't have time, Lloyd. It needs to be done now. We can't wait for Marcus or any of the others to come back here to collect it. Just tell me what I need to do."

Again, Lloyd looked deeply concerned.

"You know I'm right. If we wait any longer then we're all dead anyway."

He shook his head as he acquiesced. "You have to get it onto the tank somehow, preferably on top of it. Then shoot it with your highest weapon setting." He lifted up the stubby cylinder and moved it around in his hands. "Now if we had a way to make it stick, you might get away with just throwing it."

Another rumble echoed around the hangar, and they all instinctively ducked a little.

Mia grabbed the unit. "No time. I'll figure something out."

There's a stairway at the back of the hangar." Lloyd pointed. "It will take you to the rooftop. Be careful—at the far end, that's where the dome wall comes down. You don't want that thing detonating close to the dome."

Mia nodded.

"I'll tell Marcus to expect you, get you some backup."

"Okay," she said with a certain resignation. "Wish me luck."

"Good luck." Lloyd raised a hand as she sped off to find her way up to the rooftop.

18

SPIDER TANK

Mia stuffed the device inside her jacket and unclipped her plasma weapon as she exited onto the roof of the warehouse. The edge of the vast dome that enclosed most of this sector seemed to be only a hand's reach away—on the other side of which the mother of all dust storms endlessly raged, mirrored now by the storm playing itself out across the city. Another boom, much louder this time, reverberated off the great dome's surface and almost deafened Mia and she spun around to look for its source.

The rooftop was a maze of ducts and air filtration systems that facilitated the double-skinned approach to the city's building codes. The vast outer dome being the first, the internal buildings and physical infrastructure within being the second line of life support. Should the dome be breached, then the citizens could seek sanctuary within the buildings. At least, that was the theory. But the endless dust storm had undermined that design. With consistent system failure and the shortage of spare parts, it was all they could do just to maintain the integrity of the outer dome, and even that could not fully keep the incessant dust at bay. So much so that Mia could not see all the way across to the other side of the great dome, just a tangled mess of rooftops disappearing into a thick, murky fog.

Plasma fire split the haze, and Mia oriented herself to head for its source. She picked her way across the roof and saw Anka running over to her out of the gloom.

"Over here. Quick, quick." Mia could see she was breathing hard, even though her dust mask dulled the sound of her voice. They kept low and inched their way to the edge of the building. The sounds of the battle grew louder as they approached. The area was thick with the smell of ozone as the plasma weapons ionized the air. Mia crouched down using a squat industrial unit as cover. Anka did the same as she proceeded to map out the battle.

"The tank's around fifty meters that way." She pointed with the muzzle of her weapon. "Marcus and the main group are up on the other side, over there. We've got several buildings collapsed between us and them. There's another group at street level, but they're boxed in."

"Okay, I get the general picture. Anyone else here with you?"

Anka's face took on a pained expression. "No, I'm all that's left here."

"Milo?"

She shook her head and looked away. "He was on that building there when it was hit and collapsed. I don't know if he's still alive."

Mia said nothing. There was nothing to say. What she needed—what they all needed—was for her to take this machine down before it killed them all. Mia carefully crawled her way to the edge of the rooftop and peeked over.

The street below was a scene of pure carnage. Whole buildings had simply crumpled, and many of those that still stood were scorched and blackened. Bodies were scattered all along the street, interspersed with the wreckage of ground cars and containers.

Up ahead, the massive asteroid mining machine moved through thick, billowing smoke as plasma fire raked it from both sides of the street. More weapons fire was returned from the Montecristo security following along behind.

"Holy crap." Mia had not truly visualized the sheer size of the mechanical beast that was slowly pushing its way toward her. On the feeds it had seemed less intimidating. But now, face-to-face, so to speak, it evoked a deep, primordial response in her, a kind of long-dormant evolutionary fear, one reserved for creatures that walked around on eight legs—arachnids.

"I hate spiders," she said. More to herself than to Anka, who had now crouched down beside her.

Mia studied it for a moment, trying to figure out how

she might get the incendiary device attached. The machine was slow and ponderous, made more so by two of its legs having been damaged. Its forward-facing body was armored, presumably to protect it from any debris generated by its ballistic weapon. Yet this was not a military weapon; it was designed to work on the surface of asteroids, engineered for operation in the vacuum of space. It was also hardened against cosmic radiation, making it virtually impervious to both EMP and pulsed energy weapons. Nevertheless, it did have its vulnerabilities, and that was its lack of physical armor on all but the front-facing section of the machine.

For Mia to have any chance of bringing this thing down, she would need to get high up and try to lob the incendiary device down into the exposed engineering on its topside. She scanned the roofline for a suitable attack position. She needed to hurry; the machine was moving ever closer, and it would soon be too late.

"Anka, I'm going to try to get up on top of that cooling tower over there." She pointed off to a two-meter-high structure jutting up from the roofline. "When the spider comes alongside, I'm going to lob this into it. Then I need lots of firepower directed at it so it detonates. Can you contact Marcus and the others, get me some cover so I can reach that tower?"

"Sure, can do."

"And tell them to pass on the message that once I throw this in, they need to focus all their weapons on it."

Anka cupped a hand over her earpiece and started

talking. Mia wasn't sure what she was saying, as a building across the street crumpled under another explosion.

Mia got herself into a crouch, ready to move. Anka gave her the thumbs-up as a hail of plasma fire started raining down on the Montecristo security following the tank. She took her opportunity and ran for the cooling tower, dodging the returning fire from the security contingent down on the street. She made her way to the back of the tower and clambered up a metal ladder. Mia spread herself flat on the roof and eased her way to the edge. From this vantage point, she had a good view of the battle down below.

The spider tank was now directly beneath her and in the process of orienting itself to fire directly on the warehouse where the rebels had made their base, and where Lloyd now worked to retrieve the information held in Gizmo's datastack.

Mia pulled the incendiary device from inside her jacket and looked over to where Anka had taken up a concealed position. She was watching Mia intently, waiting for the moment when Mia lobbed the device into the tank. She gave her the thumbs-up. Mia nodded back and took aim.

But she must have been spotted, as a bolt of plasma hit the tower just as she released the device. The tower's metal casing buzzed and snapped as the energy from the shot dissipated. Even though Mia was not hit directly, she still felt her nerves jangle and her muscles spasm as the residual charge rippled through her body. In the mayhem, she lost sight of the device's trajectory. *Shit, did I miss?* she thought as she fought to get control of her body and regain some motor function.

As the worst effects of the plasma pulse receded, she was able to move enough to look down at the spider tank. She scanned the machine and the surrounding area, trying to find where the incendiary device had landed. Then she spotted it, wedged between two structural ribs on the back of the tank. With a Herculean effort, she unclipped her plasma weapon and started firing at it.

The others could now see where she was aiming, and those that had a clear view also started firing, including Anka.

The device ignited in a brilliant white flash. Mia shielded her eyes, as the light was intense. It burned like a small sun, spitting out hot globs of molten metal in all directions.

The tank stopped moving. One of its spindly legs gave way, then another, and finally it crashed down to the ground and lay still as the ball of burning metal wedged in its gut grew smaller and smaller. A huge cheer rose up all around.

The security forces that had been using the underside of the tank for cover now found themselves exposed to attack from the rebels, who had the high ground. Realizing the situation they were now in, their bravado seemed to crumble, and they beat a hasty retreat back down the street, the rebels firing after them.

Mia slowly stood up on top of the cooling tower, and the rebels raised their weapons to her and cheered.

VANCE BAPTISTE WATCHED the destruction of the spider tank from a makeshift operations room that had been hastily assembled in the cargo hold of a large transport rover. He was not happy.

"What the hell just happened?" His voice was tinged with frustration.

His head of security didn't answer; he was too busy trying to get a handle on the situation. He hopped from one terminal to another, then back to the central holo-table, which displayed the battle for the maintenance sector in real time, all while the assembled techs shouted out status reports. "Asset down... Contingent withdrawing... Awaiting orders..."

Baptiste didn't really need an answer; he could see very well what was happening. That bitch Sorelli was living up to her reputation and throwing a very large spanner in his carefully laid plans.

"Talk to me, Orban." Baptiste's voice now betrayed his anger.

He had taken a shuttle down to the surface of Mars from his private orbital a few hours ago, setting it down around three kilometers from the edge of the city. He had then transferred to this rover, which had been hastily retrofitted as an operations center. It currently sat just inside the maintenance sector, as close to the battle as Orban deemed safe.

Baptiste had wanted to get closer, "to see the sweat on their foreheads," as he had put it. But the head of security had chosen to be more cautious. Just as well, as their forces were in retreat, having lost their big advantage: the tank that was now a smoking ruin.

"They fashioned some sort of incendiary device, the spider tank is dead, our personnel are retreating under fire," said Orban as he scanned the incoming data.

"Goddammit, where the hell did they get that?"

Orban just shrugged.

"Well, the decision has been made for us." Baptiste's voice was calmer now, more certain. "We do what I suggested at the very outset. Had we done that at the start, then it would be all over by now."

Orban took a step back from Baptiste and raised a hand. "I would not advise that option. The potential for innocent people to die makes it too much of a risk."

Baptiste's face grew stern. "Since when do you care? Remember, this is a war, and innocent people die all the time in war."

Orban lowered his head a little and shook it. "I don't like it. It's just too...extreme."

"Bullshit. We've no other option."

"We're going to need approval from the board of Montecristo before implementing that option."

Baptiste's face curled into barely concealed rage. He took a step toward his head of security and stabbed a finger at him. "I don't need board approval for anything. So, stop stalling and let's get this done." He lowered his finger and relaxed a little. "Alternatively, you go find another job."

Orban considered his boss for a moment, then shrugged. "It seems we have no other choice." His voice was low, conciliatory, that of a man who knew when he was beaten.

"Good. Then give the order for everyone to leave the sector. Give them thirty minutes, then seal the doors. After that we start evacuating the internal atmosphere." He jabbed a finger at Orban. "This time, no one is getting out alive."

"We'll need to let MLOD know, give them time to get out any people they have in that sector." He turned to Baptiste. "And the chief ain't going to like this."

"You just get it started. I'll deal with Becker."

"THIS IS GOING TOO FAR. I got people in there, as well as agents from Jezero. What the hell am I going to say to them?" Chief Joshua T. Becker was borderline apoplectic.

"Not my problem, Joshua," said Baptiste. "You'll just have to think of something, because this is happening. Say what you like to them, just get your people out of there."

"Goddammit, I'm already getting it in the ear from Poe Tarkin. We should at least warn them, give Sorelli and that rabble a chance to surrender. That way we can say we tried." Becker's voice was pleading.

Baptiste thought about this for a moment. "Okay, here's what we do. We broadcast an alert that, due to rebel activity in the maintenance sector, the outer dome has been compromised. Decompression alerts will activate in thirty minutes, and the sector doors will seal soon after. That will get everybody out. And we blame it all on Lloyd and his group of reactionary scum."

"That...could work." Becker was beginning to calm down now.

"In fact, I could also broadcast that appeal directly to the rebels, make it seem like we're doing the right thing by offering them a way out."

"Yes, that would be better."

"Okay," said Baptiste. "Get me a comms link to Sorelli and we'll broadcast it. If they don't take the offer, then it will be on their heads. Nobody can accuse us of not trying."

"Very well, just don't seal the doors until I have my people out."

"Well you better get on it, then. And get me that link."

19

DECOMPRESSION

Every nerve ending in Mia's body still jangled as Anka helped her down from the cooling tower. Her muscles ached where they had gone into spasm when the tower was hit. But she was buoyed up by the destruction of the spider tank, and the adrenaline pumping in her body helped mitigate against the dull background pain. And she was recovering fast; by the time she and Anka had reached the floor of the warehouse, Mia was walking unaided.

Already, some of the fighters had returned, and there was a mix of joy and sorrow in their faces. Joy for what Mia had done in destroying the spider tank, and sorrow for those they had lost. Once Anka was happy that Mia needed no more help, she took her leave to go and search for Milo in the rubble of the battle.

Lloyd saw Mia approaching first and raised a fist in

the air. A cheer went up as the others realized she was still alive. Lloyd waved to her, then pointed at something. From out behind a stack of crates, Gizmo whizzed into view. The robot waved an arm. "Greetings, Mia. It seems I have risen from the dead yet again."

"Gizmo, you're back." Mia ran over and put two arms around the droid in an uncharacteristic display of emotion. It must have been the near-death experience up on the warehouse roof that had her so off guard.

"Mia," said Gizmo, "I do believe you are actually pleased to see me."

"Do you still have the data from the search we did of the Leighton waystation?"

"I think you only love me for my data." Gizmo feigned umbrage.

Mia looked at Lloyd, who stood beside them. "What have you done to it? I swear it's becoming more human every time it's reanimated."

"I have to admit, this new power source that Lloyd kindly retrofitted is most invigorating. I feel like a young droid again." Gizmo did a quick 360-degree spin.

Mia looked from Lloyd to Gizmo and back again. Lloyd just shrugged. "It's your droid."

"And yes, I still have all the data," Gizmo finally revealed.

"Then we need to act now and get this information broadcast. With the Montecristo security forces in retreat, we can turn the tide on this battle and get the people on our side."

"We've the comms all set up, ready to go." Lloyd pointed over to the desk. "All I need to do is make the data interface with the droid."

There was a commotion at the entrance to the hangar as Marcus and his crew returned. His leg looked bloodied, and he walked with the aid of a makeshift crutch. They also wore the scars of battle. Marcus caught Mia's eye. "You did good out there, real good. I think we have the beating of them now."

Mia nodded. "Thanks, but the war isn't over yet. Not until we get the message out."

"Okay, we're nearly ready," said Lloyd. "We're just getting the last of the data dump from the droid."

Mia glanced over to where Gizmo had parked itself. A bunch of wires trailed out from an interface port on its breast casing and trailed along the floor to a bank of terminals. Several techs sat watching a stream of data cascading down monitor screens. On one, Mia could see the video feed Gizmo had taken during their search of the waystation.

One of the monitors suddenly flickered, and the stream of data stopped cascading. In its place was the MLOD logo. The tech overseeing this terminal cupped one hand over his right ear. "Boss, incoming broadcast alert from central."

Everyone in the warehouse stopped what they were doing and focused their attention on the tech. A broadcast alert from central only meant one thing: major systems failure—usually life support.

"What's it saying?" Lloyd shouted over to the tech.

The screen started to flash a warning symbol, followed by a steam of text.

"Decompression alert...maintenance sector."

An audible shock rippled through the assembled group.

"It says..." the tech continued, "the outer sector dome has sustained significant damage due to recent insurgent activity. Losing atmosphere at an unsustainable rate. Evacuation alert imminent."

"This is bullshit," said Marcus. "There's no damage to the dome. It would take a nuke to put a dent in it."

Outside, all across the sector, sirens began to wail, rising in pitch until they split the air with an ear-piercing shrill. It was the decompression alarm, a sound that struck fear into every person who had ever lived in a pressurized environment.

"Shit, this is real," said one of the fighters. "We got to get out."

"Bullshit. They're lying," said another. "No way this sector is losing atmosphere."

Lloyd was now over at the terminal, studying data readouts. "Actually, we are. There's a minor drop in pressure." He looked up from the screen at the others. "And it's falling." He went back to the readout. "At this rate, I estimate we have twenty-seven minutes before isolation."

"Isolation?" It was a term that awoke a deep-rooted emotional trauma in Mia, as her mind went back to the incident in the agri-dome in Jezero.

"It means the sector doors close, isolating this area so that the other sectors are not compromised."

"It means we have less that twenty-seven minutes to get out or slowly die by hypoxia."

"They must be doing this—Montecristo," said an adamant Marcus. "They're controlling the air pressure. There's no damage to the dome."

"It's possible," said Lloyd. "They do control all the infrastructure, so they could do it, but they would need buy-in from MLOD. How is that possible?"

"What do we do?" said Marcus. "We can't fight this."

"We do what we planned to do all along," said Mia. "We get this data out to the people."

"Then we don't have much time," said Lloyd.

"Boss, incoming comms," a tech shouted over from a terminal. She had one hand cupped over her right ear, listening to something as a comms alert flashed on her terminal screen.

"Who is it?" Lloyd answered.

The tech swung around on her chair and looked wide-eyed at them. "Eh...I think it's Vance Baptiste. He wants to talk to Major Sorelli."

All eyes turned to Mia.

"Baptiste?" Mia considered what this might mean. "Can we record it? Better yet, can we broadcast it?"

The tech looked to Lloyd for guidance, unsure of how to answer.

"We can, can't we?" Lloyd prompted.

The tech nodded. "Yeah, we can do both...with a slight delay. A few seconds."

"Okay, get it set up. I'll take the call." Mia moved over to the terminal. "Put a camera on me, but make sure there's nothing in the background we don't want them to see."

It took the tech and Lloyd less than a minute to get set up. Mia stood facing the terminal, which had now been elevated and oriented so the background was just...empty space. Mia nodded, and the tech made the comms connection.

On screen, the head and shoulders of Vance Baptiste materialized. In the background, several techs could be seen arrayed along a bank of terminals, presumably an operations center. And if Mia was not mistaken, it looked to be the interior of an industrial transport rover. Also in the background, looking away from the camera, was the unmistakable figure of Orban Dent, Montecristo's head of security, still wearing his long black coat.

Baptiste spoke. "Ah...Major Mia Sorelli. What a pain in the ass you're turning out to be."

"Glad to be of service," Mia was quick to reply. "So, I presume you want to say sorry for the destruction caused to the maintenance sector by Montecristo Industries, and offer reparations?"

"Ha, ha... Good to see that you've retained a sense of humor, considering that you're now a wanted terrorist. The MLOD in Jezero are anxious to see you brought to justice, along with the other criminals you're consorting with."

"You mean the citizens who are attempting to expose Montecristo's theft of vital spare parts—components that could have saved the lives of a great many people."

Baptiste let a snort. "Enough of this bullshit. I'm here to give you all an offer. Not my idea, I assure you, but it would seem that you still have some hold over the council of Mars back in Jezero, and since they have kindly lent their support in our efforts to crush this little uprising of yours, I owe them one. So here it is."

He took a breath. "No doubt you have noticed there is an area-wide alert just issued from central, indicating that the sector dome has been damaged by terrorists— that would be you—and that the sector is now losing atmosphere."

Mia couldn't stop herself from crying foul. "And we know it's bullshit. It's Montecristo Industries who are doing this."

"If you and your comrades were to surrender now, then the decompression alert will magically fix itself. There's no need for innocent people in the maintenance sector to die. So, I suggest you do the right thing."

"Does Chief Becker know what you're doing?"

"Becker knows which side he's on. Law and order needs to be maintained."

"At any cost?"

"That's your choice. Personally, I rather hope you

don't take the offer, as I would rather see you dead. But maybe there is still a way for that to happen—even if you do."

"Like you did with Agent Dan Frazer?"

"He was a fool, and like you he stuck his nose into places that were none of his business."

Mia glanced over at Lloyd and nodded. That was her signal for them to start broadcasting the conversation.

"You mean because of what he found out?"

Baptiste gave a laugh. "Ha, is that what you think?" He leaned into the camera. "You and your bunch of merry men and women are all that's between Montecristo Industries and control of that sector. And with that gives us control of the council, and with that gives us all of Mars. So, it's time to grow up and realize just how out of your league you really are."

"So that's what all the stockpiling was for, all those crates of vital components you've been stealing and hoarding. Just so you can take control. All those people who didn't need to die, all the systems failures that didn't need to happen."

"Your time is up. The choice is yours."

"Well, here's what I'm going to do: Arrest your head of security for the murder of Agent Dan Frazer, and you for crimes against the state."

Baptiste let out a long, genuine laugh. "Ha-ha... I've got to hand it to you, Sorelli, you do have a great sense of humor." His focus flipped away from the camera as Orban grabbed his attention and pointed to something off camera. They had just realized that it was all being broadcast, along with the video feed from the Leighton waystation.

He swung his head back to the camera, and his face had screwed itself into one of barely controlled rage. "You won't get away with this. You'll pay..." The connection terminated.

Mia looked over at Lloyd. "Did it get out?"

"Yes, all of it. The conversation, the video from the waystation, the data, everything."

"Any reaction?"

"Yes, but the picture is very confused." One of the techs scanned an array of real-time feeds. "We've got counter-comments from MLOD and Montecristo, some indications of people taking to the streets, and some people are panicking. It's a bit of a mess."

"It's going to take time. Just keep repeating the broadcast," said Mia.

"It won't take them long to block it," said Marcus. "Then what?"

"Hopefully it will have done its damage by then. In the meantime, we've got fifteen minutes to get out of here."

"I'm not going," said Lloyd.

"We don't have a choice," Mia pleaded. "If we stay, we die."

"Boss, the doors are starting to close. I'm getting reports of panic at the exits, people trying to get out."

"I don't believe it," said Marcus. "How can they do this?"

"Are you sure?" Lloyd turned to the tech.

"The reports are very confused. But it seems panic has set in. Wait a minute..." The tech raised a hand for silence so she could concentrate, then swung around on her seat and looked at them. "They're putting all the other sectors under Montecristo control into lockdown. Nobody can move around the city."

"Shit, can they do that?" said Mia.

"It would appear so," replied the tech.

"This is getting way out of hand," said one of the fighters. "We've only made things worse."

"Bullshit," said another. "We're not the people pulling the levers on this. It's Baptiste who's giving the orders. He's the one putting every citizen's life in danger."

"Twelve minutes," the tech called out.

"Let's face it, we're not getting out." Marcus slumped down on a crate. "How long have we got once the doors close?"

"Hard to say." Lloyd was now checking readouts. "Depends on how fast they suck all the air out. The sector dome has a vast volume, so it could be many hours, maybe even days."

"And we can't stop it. With all the other sectors going into lockdown, there's no way to get people onto the streets, no matter how riled up they are." Marcus winced as he stretched his injured leg out.

"I can't believe that the MLOD and Jezero are just

going to sit back and let this happen," said Mia. "Can we contact them? Try to persuade them to take action, do the right thing?"

"Worth a shot." Lloyd turned to one of the comms techs. "Can you try to get a connection?"

The tech's fingers danced across the control interface. Eventually she just shook her head. "No joy, we've been shut out. No outside comms, all dead."

There was a moment of silence in the warehouse as the seriousness of the situation began to sink in. Evacuating may not be that simple; if the citizens were panicking and trying to push through the exit routes, people would get hurt in the clamor to get out. Staying, on the other hand, would be a long, slow death.

"How are they doing this? Where are they controlling it from?" Mia directed her question at Lloyd, who was now over at the comms desk, trying to find out how they were being blocked.

"They control the systems, they have the power." Lloyd waved a hand dismissively, and Mia could see a sense of frustration beginning to affect him.

"No, I mean where from? Do they have a central operations center?"

Lloyd stood up from the comms desk, seeming to accept defeat. He could not find a comms route out. He sighed and turned to face Mia. "Yes, somewhere. But what does it matter?"

"Where?"

"Over at their HQ, industrial sector. But there's no way we can get there."

"Yes there is." Mia turned and pointed at the maintenance airlock, way at the back of the hangar. "You're forgetting—we still have a rover."

Lloyd's eyes widened as the realization sank in. "You're not seriously thinking of trying to get into their HQ?"

"Sounds like a good idea to me," said Marcus.

Some of the others had now picked up on Mia's plan and began to gather around.

"It could give us a chance," said one.

"Better than staying here," said another.

"But think about what you're proposing, Mia," said Lloyd. "Even if you do manage to get there, how are you going to hack your way through their security?"

A thin smile broke across her face, and she turned to the comms desk. "Gizmo, fancy another adventure?"

"Absolutely. I am beginning to get a bit bored here anyway." The droid detached the cables that had been connected to it for the data transfer and whizzed over beside Mia. "When do we start?"

"Wait a minute, let's think about this." Lloyd raised a hand in a halting gesture.

"Nothing to think," said Marcus. "Let her do this."

"Seven minutes," the techs shouted out.

Lloyd turned to the assembled fighters. "Everybody, it's time to get out of here. We've got seven minutes until lockdown. We fought the good fight, but it's over. Go now, while there's still a chance to come out of this alive."

But already their numbers had thinned out. Some had left as soon as the decompression alert sounded, its shrill whine still audible. Now more drifted off, leaving a small cohort of die-hards—those who would fight to the last. Those who would see it out to the bitter end.

But there were also quite a few who were injured in the fighting. They were stuck here, whether they liked it or not. One of those was Milo.

Anka had found him, still alive and buried under a mound of crumpled metal. His leg was broken, his left shoulder dislocated, he had burns and scorch marks all over his torso—he was not going anywhere, and neither was Anka.

"Look, we've got people injured. None of them are getting out. So, let's not waste any more time or people." Mia turned to Lloyd. "Let me and Gizmo do this. Just tell us, how do we find this place?"

"All I need are the coordinates," said Gizmo. "I can navigate, and I can also find the best route in."

Lloyd looked around at the injured who had been laid out on the floor of the hangar and made as comfortable as possible. "I should stay here. If Gizmo can navigate and hack his way in, then I'll just get in the way."

"I also have the advantage of not dying when exposed to the vacuum of space," said Gizmo.

Lloyd pursed his lips and slowly raised one finger. "Actually, there may be another way."

"Four minutes."

"Can you knock that off?" Marcus shouted over at the tech, a little harshly. "Do we really want to know?"

"A better way?" said Mia.

"It's a distributed system. Meaning we don't necessarily need to gain access to Montecristo HQ. Control can be accessed from multiple locations—all you need is the right terminal and the authority."

"You mean we could hack in from here?"

"No, no. That's not possible. It uses quantum encryption, so any terminal won't do—we need a specific terminal. But there are any number of them throughout the Montecristo network."

"Do you know where they are? Is there one we can get to without having to shoot our way into HQ?"

"I'm certain there's one in that rover that Baptiste was operating from, and that would have less security around it than HQ."

Mia thought for a moment. This possibility was tempting. Going after Baptiste and Orban would be a real coup, if she could pull it off. "Any ideas where it is?"

Lloyd smiled. "Yes, I know exactly where it is. At least, where it was when they made the comms connection. I ran a trace on its location. Baptiste was so cocksure of himself that he didn't think to block it."

"Gizmo, do you know where it is? Can you navigate there?"

"I can get us to the last known position. We will need to exit onto the planet surface and then reenter the city on the outskirts of the maintenance sector. But there is a high probability it has moved from that location."

"We'll take that chance." Mia turned to go.

"Good luck," said Lloyd. "I'll try and get comms reestablished. Maybe we can contact MLOD or Jezero."

Mia nodded and headed off to the rover with Gizmo by her side.

20

MLOD HQ

Chief Joshua T. Becker stood in front of a wall of monitors in the situation room of the MLOD HQ in Syrtis. He held his head in both hands, his mouth was open, and his eyes were almost popping out of his skull as he contemplated the mayhem unfolding all across the city. His mind was finding it extremely difficult to absorb the scale of the social disintegration that was now developing. Why had he ever allowed that slimeball Vance Baptiste to talk him into this? Becker knew he was going to burn for this catastrophe, and burn bad.

The broadcast of Montecristo's duplicity by Major Sorelli had opened a valve in the city, and all the pent-up frustrations of a population living on the edge had come flooding out. But then again, over 380 sols of slowly disintegrating life support and infrastructure will do that to

GERALD M KILBY

people. When there is seemingly no hope, only a steady slide into extinction, the citizens will eventually start to get angry. Very, very angry.

Before this, that frustration had simply manifested itself in protests, demonstrations, social unrest, and some acts of violence and vandalism. It had been this level of unrest that the MLOD and their security contractors Montecristo had been dealing with for the last few months—and only just keeping a lid on things. Now it had escalated into all-out war, and that war had just piled on to the streets and found a target: Montecristo Industries.

Where before, the frustration of the populace had had no real focus other than raging against the eternal dust storm encircling the planet, now, they had found a target, one they saw as exacerbating the misery wrought on the people by denying them the very supplies they needed to survive. And their collective rage knew no bounds.

In every sector across the city, locked down or not, people piled onto the streets and began attacking any facility or asset that had anything to do with Montecristo Industries. The only thing holding them back from tearing these assets to shreds were the combined MLOD officers of Syrtis and Jezero. But Chief Joshua T. Becker knew that this would not be enough; they could not hold back this rage much longer, and the situation was now critical. The dam was bursting, and it threatened to bring about the total destruction of the city and everyone in it.

"You know, all she had to do was bring back Agent Frazer's body."

Becker was jolted out of his near catatonic state by a voice beside him. He looked around. It was the director of planetary security, Poe Tarkin. He had taken the shuttle from Jezero along with the newly arrived contingent of officers.

"But no, instead she had to unleash Armageddon," Poe continued.

Becker didn't bother to reply. He just went back to watching the violence unfold all across Syrtis.

"Did you know anything about this?" said Tarkin after a moment.

"What?" Becker looked at him, a little annoyed.

"About Montecristo siphoning off components from the aid shipments?"

Becker found the question almost irrelevant. *What does it matter now?* he thought. The damage had been done, and there was no going back. He gave a dismissive grunt and looked back at the screens for a moment before sighing again. "Yes, I did. We all did. But not the extent to which they were doing it. We all turned a blind eye to what we presumed was some minor...*redirection* of resources." He waved an arm to indicate he was referring to the other MLOD officers in HQ. "We felt it a small price to pay for Montecristo's continued involvement in local law enforcement."

"And this...vendetta against the people in the mainte-nance sector?" Poe pressed.

Becker rubbed a thick bead of sweat from his forehead. "Bottom line was, we needed them, needed their manpower and technology, and they knew that." He looked at Poe with a pained, tortured expression on his face. "It just became harder and harder to say no. What choice did I have?"

"There's always a choice, Joshua." Tarkin lowered his head a little and shook it. "Well, what's done is done. And if Major Sorelli is right about the extent of the crime, then a lot of people didn't have to die."

"Too late now. And if we don't do something soon, then a lot more people are going to die."

Becker turned his attention to one of the techs. "Any word from that bastard Baptiste?"

"No, sir. Nothing."

"Or the Montecristo board?"

"No, sir. Just the same statement as before."

The corporation's board had simply issued a bland statement on the unfolding situation. *We are shocked to learn of the illegal activities of Vance Baptiste. You can be assured that this corruption will be rooted out. We are every bit as concerned as the MLOD and are monitoring the situation closely.*

"Really? Well that's just great then, isn't it? Nothing to worry about."

"Agent Frazer was investigating this, wasn't he?"

Becker threw his hands up in the air in exasperation. "What are you saying, Poe?"

"I get the feeling, Joshua, that you know more about what went on than you're admitting."

"Fuck you. You're not the one trying to keep Syrtis from disintegrating. It's okay for you in Jezero. You don't have the population we have—four hundred thousand desperate people, all ready to explode. Jezero is a bastion of civilized culture compared to here. So spare me the condescension, Poe."

"The law is the law, Joshua. You should know this—you're the chief of police."

"These are desperate times, Poe. We do what we need to do. Who are you to judge?"

Poe Tarkin looked away and returned his attention to the unfolding drama on screen. "Perhaps you're right, Joshua. Now is not the time for moral analysis. Now is the time to take action. We will be remembered for what we do now more than for what has gone before." He turned back to the chief. "What I'd like to know is, whose side are you on?"

Becker gave him a hard stare, then jabbed a finger at him. "The side I've always been on—the people of Syrtis. Montecristo and that vile bastard Vance Baptiste have played us all for fools, me more so than most. Okay, I'll admit it, I was wrong." He turned to face the screens as his body visibly deflated. "The thing is, Poe, I really don't know what to do."

"We give the people what they want, which is justice," said Poe, a little pompously for Becker's liking. "That means us taking control of this situation. So, here's what we do. First, tell Montecristo they must hand over all the components that they've...stolen. We will send a contingent out to the Leighton waystation to oversee handover. Then we broadcast it, just like Major Sorelli did. That should start getting the people on our side. We do that, along with copious appeals for calm.

"Next, we need Vance Baptiste's head. Because someone needs to pay, and be seen to pay. And that's Baptiste. Therefore, Montecristo will need to play ball. If they've a problem handing him over, then we threaten to withdraw all our officers from protecting Montecristo facilities, let the mob tear them all to shreds."

Becker looked at the director of planetary security. "What about Sorelli, and all those in the maintenance sector?"

Poe Tarkin thought for a moment. "Try to make contact with Agent Sorelli or that Lloyd guy. They'll have a better idea of what's really going on in there."

Becker nodded. "Okay, I'll get some people on it right away."

THE SUDDENNESS of the reaction to the rebels' broadcast, and the sheer scale of it, came as a shock to Vance Baptiste. So sure had he been of his plan to rid Montecristo of the threat that Mia Sorelli posed, and to finally acquire control of the problematic maintenance sector, that he was now having trouble believing it was all going to rat-shit. Already, Montecristo assets were under attack in every sector, and now relied more than ever on the assistance of the MLOD to keep the mob at bay.

The evacuation of the maintenance sector had turned into chaos, but at least that was now fully locked down, and soon all resistance still remaining inside would be dead. Then Montecristo could walk right in and take control. So it wasn't all bad. Just so long as the MLOD held the line, then he could still pull this off. Nevertheless, neither he nor Orban were taking any chances. They decided that it would be best if they moved the rover they were using as a base of operations outside the city, onto the planet's surface. Out there, it would be difficult for anyone to threaten them. They would wait it out for however long it took for things to settle down before reentering Syrtis again.

They had taken it out via the northern airlock gate and parked up around two kilometers from the city's edge, very near to where their shuttle was still parked. But comms was being severely disrupted by the intense ionization of the dust storm, and the techs failed to establish any coherent signals. Finally, after several attempts to rectify the issue, they decided it would just be easier to move the rover back closer to the city's edge, where the signal would be stronger.

They were now bumping their way back across the

surface, around half a kilometer from the metropolis, when the comms gear finally kicked back into life. Almost immediately, the holo-table in the center of the operation bay blossomed to life, and a 3D, rotating Montecristo Industries logo hovered above its surface.

"Sir, the board over at HQ are requesting a conference connection."

"Excellent, please proceed. You can bring it up on the holo-table." Baptiste had assumed the board were contacting him so that they could congratulate him on the operation. As they should, considering the amount of time and resources he had invested in this entire operation.

The logo on the holo-table gracefully disassembled itself and several avatars began to materialize, one for each member of the Montecristo Industries board.

The session began with the avatar identified as the Chair. "We have convened the board for a special meeting to discuss the current situation developing in Syrtis."

"Very good," said Baptiste enthusiastically. "My apologies for the poor quality of communications. We are currently outside the city." He waved a hand in the air. "The dust storm plays havoc with the telemetry."

"Where exactly are you located? The coordinates, please?" said the Chair.

Baptiste considered this an odd request. Why were they so interested in his exact location? One of the techs looked over at him and nodded. Baptiste looked back at the board of avatars. "I believe that has now been sent."

"Very good."

The corporation's CEO now spoke up. "The situation on the ground is becoming...problematic, and a significant proportion of our facilities are under attack from mobs of irate citizens."

"It will pass," said Baptiste. "Just hold the line."

"That's a strategy we may have difficulty implementing, as the MLOD have decided to grow a set of balls and are demanding we hand over the entire contents of Leighton waystation, or they will withdraw their officers." The CEO could barely conceal his frustration.

"They're bluffing." Baptiste waved a dismissive hand in the air. "They know as well as anyone that our facilities are the only thing keeping life support functioning in this city."

The CTO now chimed in. "Perhaps, but officers from Jezero have already withdrawn and are heading out to Leighton."

"We may have had a hold over Chief Becker, but Poe Tarkin is another matter," said the CEO to another of the avatars. "He is proving to be serious in his threat."

"Let him try," Baptiste interjected.

There was a brief moment of disconcerting silence as the board members began discussing something amongst themselves. Finally, the Chair turned to Baptiste. "Given these...unfortunate developments, the board have come to a view on how best to proceed. Please understand that we have not come to this lightly. It's just...well, business."

Baptiste did not like the sound of this—not one bit.

"We agree to hand over the stockpile of components to the officers of the MLOD in return for their guarantee of continued security provision."

"No way. I disagree totally," said Baptiste. "Those components are what has enabled us to buy the loyalty of the citizens."

"Any goodwill shown toward Montecristo Industries by the locals has all but evaporated after that...charade was broadcast." The CEO began to underscore the board's decision. "No amount of us fixing things up is going to buy that back. It's gone for good. This is now a damage limitation exercise."

"But..."

"But nothing. This is the way it is. We hand the components over, and then do a public relations campaign to show just how generous we are in these...challenging times. It's not going to get us back to where we were, but at least it might calm things down."

Baptiste was not liking where this was going. "We are very close to gaining complete control. The maintenance sector will be ours soon, and that has always been the last piece in the jigsaw."

"It's too late now," the CEO continued. "We've lost a significant amount of goodwill. Not even control of the sector will make up for that loss. Therefore, we demand that you reverse the evacuation protocol, take it out of lockdown."

"What? After all I've done to get us to this point? This is...is treason."

The board erupted in a chorus of outrage at this accusation from Baptiste. "You are way out of order. We're trying to save what we can from the mess that *you* have created." The Chair pointed an angry finger directly at him.

Baptiste was beginning to smell a rat. They were turning on him, and the question uppermost in his mind now was *how far would that go?* Would they go as far as to abandon both him and Orban? Was it possible that, far from being heralded as a hero, he would now be thrown to the wolves? What was really in the deal they hatched with the MLOD? Did it include handing them his head on a plate?

"And where does that leave me in all of this?" he finally said.

The board shuffled and shifted around uncomfortably. Even though they were just 3D avatars floating above the holo-table, he could still sense their collective unease at this question. It was at that moment he realized they were going to shaft him.

"We can, eh...discuss that once the dust settles, so to speak. We just need you to give the authorization to reverse the evacuation of the maintenance sector and...eh, return to HQ."

There it was. As clear as day, as far as Baptiste was concerned. They were keeping the discussion polite and civil because they knew he was the only one with the authorization key to reverse the evacuation protocol.

They needed him. But once it was done, he was nothing. He would lose all power.

He thought about this for a moment and decided to play it cool. He just shrugged. "Very well, so be it. Although, I'll be honest and say that I disagree with this strategy, but if it's the decision of the board, then I'll reverse the lockdown and head for HQ." Baptiste employed his best acting skills to deliver this last line, in the hope that they would truly believe it.

The avatars' collective body language began to relax a little. "Yes, agreed. Disappointing, but it is the best way out of this...current impasse," said the CEO. The other avatars nodded in agreement.

From then on, Baptiste zoned out, and the mutterings of the board drifted into the background of his consciousness as he formulated his next move. He only came back when they were signing off.

"Yeah, sure. We can discuss again later." He cut the transmission and turned to Orban. "This is bullshit."

"Well, I told you so."

Baptiste's face reconfigured from a look of anger to one of disdain. "I'm beginning to wonder just how useful you are to me, Orban."

"I'll pretend I didn't hear that. I suggest our best option is to do what they say—reverse the evacuation and then head for HQ."

A strange, disconcerting smile cracked across Baptiste's mottled face. "Don't you think it was a bit odd, asking for our location?"

Orban just shrugged.

"The only reason they would want that is if we didn't agree to reverse the evacuation. Then, I presume, they would send a crew out here to make us comply. Which means we're no longer of any use to them. They've probably hatched a deal with MLOD for our respective heads, just so they can save face—because they are weak. They've sold us out, Orban, and lost what it was that they wanted so badly—absolute power. I could have given them that, if they only had the balls to stick it out to the bitter end. But no, they're duplicitous, only concerned now with salvaging the bottom line. So, I say we screw them, and we screw them good."

Orban remained silent for a moment, mentally digesting Baptiste's rant.

"They contracted me to do what they themselves tried so hard to do, but failed." Baptiste slapped his chest. "Now they shaft me just when the going gets tough. But here's the thing—they can't reverse the evacuation in the maintenance sector without this." Baptiste reached into a pocket and pulled out a small object, not unlike a key fob on a neck chain, and dangled it in front of Orban. "The protocol is encrypted with this key, and only it can reverse the procedure."

Orban Dent fixed his eyes on the key.

"So, I say we let it roll, and all those scumbags in there will die." Baptiste shoved the key back in his pocket. "Now, maybe Montecristo Industries can survive that. After all, the people left in there are just rebels."

Baptiste went silent for a moment, thinking. Then turned back to Orban and raised a finger in the air. "I've an even better idea. Let's say we put all Montecristo sectors into atmospheric decompression. I'd like to see them survive the fallout from that." He began to laugh.

Orban's eyes widened a little, and his face hardened. "Are you totally fucking crazy?" he managed to say through gritted teeth. "You would kill all those people just to get back at Montecristo?"

Baptiste jabbed a finger at Orban this time. "Don't start growing a moral core all of a sudden. You're pretty good at killing people when you want to."

"Not when I *want* to, only when I *have* to. There's a big difference." He shook his head. "I can't let you do this."

"What? Not you as well." He threw his hands up. "Is there some disease in the air that's turning everyone into pussies?"

Orban's face grew tighter, his eyes narrowing this time. Then he lunged, making a grab for Baptiste's neck.

But Baptiste had anticipated this move. He was a person who prided himself on his ability to see what was coming down the track. He imagined that it was a kind of superpower he possessed, to know what someone was going to do before they even knew it themselves. So, he simply sidestepped, grabbing Orban's outstretched arm as he did, and used the oncoming momentum to send him tumbling across the floor of the rover.

Orban rolled and righted himself with the agility of a

cat, but it wasn't fast enough, as Baptiste already had a plasma weapon trained on him. Orban halted.

"You're a treacherous bastard, Orban Dent. Of all the people to turn on me, I never thought it would be you."

"That was before you..." But he didn't get to finish the sentence, as a bolt of incandescent plasma hit his chest. He was slammed back against an equipment rack, then slowly slumped to the floor. A thin filament of acrid smoke wafted up from his torso.

Baptiste turned the weapon on the techs sitting at two separate terminals in the rover's operations bay. "Anybody got any questions?"

They sat stock still, eyes wide, and very delicately shook their heads to signify that they didn't.

Baptiste pocketed the weapon. "Good. Now let's get this show on the road."

He took the key fob from his pocket and inserted it into a slot on the holo-table. A detailed rendering of the entire city of Syrtis blossomed to life. It showed all sectors, but the ones that Baptiste was interested in were those controlled by Montecristo Industries. This constituted over half the city. One by one he began to initiate the protocol that would evacuate the atmosphere in each of these sectors. This would, in turn, instigate an automatic lockdown.

As he worked, dialing in the instructions, he was already considering his next move. He would head for the shuttle that he and the treacherous Orban Dent had landed in and head back up to his private orbital. There, no one could touch him. After that he might take a trip to Ceres, or maybe even return to Earth. *There's always a welcome on Earth for a man of my talents,* he thought.

All across Syrtis, decompression klaxons began to wail, and every man, woman, and child began to panic.

21

SURFACE TENSION

The wide airlock door in Lloyd's warehouse slowly opened, and a thin haze of Martian dust began to drift in from the turbulent planetary surface. Gizmo took control of the rover's operation and began to gently roll it out onto the flat concrete apron skirting the city's perimeter.

Mia sat up in the cockpit beside the droid and strained her eyes to seek out some visual definition in the fog now beginning to engulf the machine. The sun was rising, and the light had given the atmosphere a strange, ethereal quality. It was like driving into a rust-colored dreamscape; it had an eerie, transcendent beauty to it.

"We have cleared the airlock." Gizmo's voice jolted Mia out of her reverie. "I am going to take us out a little farther and then turn to follow the edge of the city. I think I have found a way back in."

With that, the central cockpit console sprang to life

and a 3D schematic of their location blossomed out of a small holo-slate. It flickered and fizzed as the exterior sensors tried to establish its location through the electrical mayhem of the dust storm. As Gizmo turned the machine, the 3D map rotated in unison.

Through the windscreen of the rover, Mia could just make out the looming shadow of the sector dome as it passed to the left of her. Ahead, she could also just make out the concrete apron that Gizmo was following. But nothing was really visible beyond a few meters; everything dissolved into a blanket of swirling dust.

After several minutes of uneventful driving following the edge of the city, the cockpit comms crackled into life. "Mia, this is Lloyd. Are you receiving me?" The voice was fuzzy and distorted. The ionized atmosphere was playing havoc with the transmission.

Mia grabbed the cockpit comms handset to reply. "Yeah, what is it?"

"There's been some developments. Baptiste has gone insane, and the entire city is in chaos."

"What do you mean, insane?"

"I'm going to patch you through to MLOD. They can explain the current situation better that I can."

Mia glanced over at Gizmo and arched an eyebrow.

"Uh-oh," said the droid. "Insane is never a good sign. Should I halt the rover and wait?"

"No, we may as well keep going."

A new voice crackled out of the cockpit comms. It

sounded familiar to Mia, but she couldn't quite put her finger on it.

"Hello, Mia."

"Who's this?"

"Poe Tarkin. I'm here in Syrtis, helping the local MLOD."

Mia gave an audible sigh. "So what do you want with me? I thought I was persona non grata?"

"The situation has changed, Mia. Now it looks like you may be our only hope."

"Really? Well now, there's a surprise. Does that mean I'm no longer a rebel outlaw?"

"Perhaps we were...eh, a bit slow to fully appreciate the gravity of the situation. So, my apologies, but we don't have much time. It appears that Vance Baptiste has lost his goddamn mind and has instigated a decompression protocol in all Montecristo Industries sectors."

"Ho-ly crap! Why would he do that?"

"After your broadcast exposing the scam they were pulling with components, the people have turned and are trying to attack their facilities. So, they made a deal with the MLOD. We're providing the security to protect their infrastructure, and they are to hand over the components, as well as Baptiste and his head of security, Orban, to us for trial. I think Baptiste's actions are his way of getting back at them."

"That's incredible."

"Baptiste must have seen it coming, so he turned the screws on them and the city, and now he's on his way back to his shuttle, presumably to escape to his private orbital. If he gets there, he's virtually untouchable."

"So, screw him. We can get him again some other time."

"The problem is he's the only one who can reverse the decompression protocols. He encrypted the authorization, so only he has control."

"I see."

"We need to find him and get the key. He carries it around his neck, or in a pocket. If we have that, we can stop this insanity."

"Where is he now?"

"En route to the shuttle. It's parked up around three kilometers outside the city, at the old shuttle port. You've got to stop him before he gets there."

"What about MLOD or Montecristo? Can they not go after him?"

"We're in lockdown, and those who are outside the affected sectors can't get there in time."

Mia gave another audible sigh. "You better give me his coordinates."

"Eh...we don't have any. All we can do is give you a best guess."

"Great. You got any idea how the hell we're going to find him out here? It's impossible to see anything in this crap."

"I know, but you are our only hope."

Mia glanced over at droid again. "You following all this, Gizmo?"

"I sure am. Looks like we are back to saving the world again."

"Yeah. Think you can find your way in this shit?" Mia waved a hand at the maelstrom outside the windscreen.

"I have limited ability to locate objects on the surface that do not have a navigation beacon. Nevertheless, I have extrapolated the possible location of Vance Baptiste's rover from last-known coordinates, probable routes to the shuttle, and the general speed of the machine. But that still gives a considerable margin of error—a radius of over a kilometer."

Mia went back to the comms. "Poe, we'll try. That's all I can say. Out."

She turned back to Gizmo and waved a hand at the dense brown fog outside the windscreen. "This is impossible. We can't see anything out there past a few meters."

"We are not completely blind," said Gizmo. "This rover does have operational range detection technology, but the dust storm greatly inhibits its performance. I estimate the effective range to be no more than three hundred meters for an object the size of Baptiste's rover."

"That'll have to do. Come on, let's get going."

Gizmo turned the rover away from the city's edge and out into the storm.

MIA WONDERED what exactly she was going to do if they managed to intercept Baptiste. How would they stop him? Ram his rover? It was an option, but a dangerous one. Their own rover could be disabled in the collision, even start to lose pressure. That would be a disaster.

She unfastened the seat harness and made her way into the back of the rover. "I'm just going to check on the old EVA suit I spotted back here. Maybe it still works."

It was hanging by the airlock door, old and battered. An industrial unit, designed for hard labor—probably mining. She booted it up and ran through some diagnostics.

The good news was it functioned. The bad was that it had limited resources. Probably not enough to get her back to safety, if she found herself outside on the planet surface and needing to walk back. But it was rugged, so it would afford her some protection. Without hesitation, she started getting suited up.

"I think I have found it!" Gizmo called out from the cockpit. "We have a sizable object traveling at speed...a little over two hundred and fifty meters away."

Mia snapped on the EVA suit helmet and made her way back to the front of the rover. She found the suit uncomfortable and way too big for her; it made her movements very awkward. It might fit better once it was pressurized, but for the moment there was no need.

"Can we intercept it?" she said as she entered the cockpit and sat down.

Gizmo looked up at Mia. "If my calculations are correct, and they always are, then it is heading straight for us—at speed."

Mia froze momentarily before flipping down her EVA suit helmet and readying her plasma weapon. "ETA?"

"One minute, eight seconds," the droid's voice reverberated over her helmet comms. "I think it might be trying to ram us. I will attempt evasive action."

"Wait, let's think. If they ram us, that means their rover will slow down or stop on impact?"

"Correct. I assume they have calculated minimal damage to their machine, otherwise they would not have countenanced this maneuver."

"So, let's get out now, onto the surface. When impact occurs, we'll have a chance to grab onto their rover, maybe find a way to disable it, or even get inside."

"That is a very reasonable plan, Mia. It may even work."

Gizmo reduced the rover's speed so that they would be able to exit through the rear airlock with minimal potential damage to Mia's EVA suit, as she would have to throw herself out rather than simply step off.

Gizmo's suspicions about the intercept intention of the other rover were also confirmed when it immediately adjusted its vector.

Mia made her way to the rear airlock, followed quickly by Gizmo, and they both squeezed themselves into the tight compartment as it cycled through its decompression routine.

The outer door opened to a sea of swirling dust kicked up by the vortex created by the rover's motion. Mia looked down at the ground moving beneath her, picked her moment, and jumped. She hit the ground harder than she had expected and was instantly glad of the protection afforded her by the rugged EVA suit. She tumbled a few meters before coming to a rest on her back, just as Gizmo materialized out of the fog.

"How did you get here so quick?" she said as she looked up at the droid.

"I was somewhat more elegant in my departure from the airlock."

The ground trembled. Mia could feel it, even through the thick EVA suit.

Gizmo's head spun around as the droid scanned the area as thick clouds of dust billowed out of the fog. "We have contact. Baptiste just rammed our rover, side on. Both rovers are currently stationary."

Mia picked herself up from the dirt and started off in the direction of the crash, Gizmo racing slightly ahead of her. "Baptiste's rover is reversing. We must hurry if we want to catch it."

A dark shadow formed in the oncoming gloom as Baptiste's rover began to materialize out from the dust. It seemed to be moving, but very slowly. Maybe it was damaged in the impact.

An incandescent ball of blue plasma burst out from near the rover and hit Mia on the left shoulder. Her suit went into cardiac arrest; readouts flickered, alerts flashed. "Shit, I've been hit. There's somebody else out on the surface." She fell to the ground and rolled over, grabbing her plasma weapon as she came around, and fired back in the direction of the first shot.

"Gizmo, catch that rover. I'll deal with the shooter."

The droid raced off toward the rover, and Mia fired several more shots to give it some level of cover. She checked her readouts; the suit had stabilized and the alerts had stopped flashing. It was a tough unit, that was for sure, and she wondered how much punishment it could actually take before giving up the ghost on her.

She stood up and ran forward. But within a few strides, another ball of plasma burst toward her. She was ready this time. She ducked the oncoming blast and fired back, three shots in quick succession. She kept running.

A moment later, she was standing over the body of a Montecristo Industries tech. His light EVA suit had a large scorch mark across his chest, a direct hit. Mia knelt and picked up the weapon lying beside him. It was high-tech, much better than her own, and could pack a considerable punch if it was dialed all the way up.

She scanned the area as best she could to try to get reoriented. There might be others out here trying to find her.

"Gizmo, where are you?"

The droid's voice crackled in her helmet. "Atop the rover, trying to detach the navigation parabola. It has already suffered damage to the front suspension from when it rammed our own rover, so it is moving slow. You can still catch it if you follow my directions."

Mia glanced around and tried to find something,

anything, in the fog that she could use as a reference point. "I can't see shit, Gizmo. It's all just sand and dust."

"I have identified your location. I need you to stand up and start moving so I can track your vector. But be warned, there is another person out there, approximately seventy-five meters away."

"Dammit." Mia again looked around, but could see nothing. She stood up slowly, keeping hunched, and moved forward.

"Okay, got you. Now head two-o'clock from your current track and you will intercept in twenty meters. The other person will be to your left."

Mia started moving as fast as she could. Within a few moments, the form of the rover began to materialize out of the fog. "I see it. I see the rover." As she came closer, she began to make out Gizmo straddling the roof of the machine just as it finally ripped the navigation parabola off the roof and flung it onto the ground.

"Watch out, Mia. Attacker fifty meters directly behind you."

Mia ducked down just as a ball of plasma came hurtling out of the dust and sailed harmlessly over her head. She took aim and fired a few bursts in the direction of the attack.

"Missed," said Gizmo. "Ten degrees left."

Mia adjusted and fired again.

"Bingo," said the droid.

She jumped up and ran for the rover. "Gizmo, I've

picked up a high-energy plasma weapon. Could I fry this machine's electronics? Would that stop it?"

"It might be worth a try, but let me get off first. I do not want to be collateral damage."

Mia watched as the droid descended the side of the rover like a monkey on speed. It dropped to the ground and raced over to Mia. "Aim just between the rear wheel assembly. That is where motor control is. That is the most vulnerable."

Mia checked the weapon and dialed it up to full power. At this level she would have just two shots, no more. She aimed and fired. The blast was blinding, and Mia had not expected the kickback from the weapon, either, so she tumbled backward onto her ass.

For one moment, the entire rear third of the rover seemed to be encased in a cage of electrical rage. Then it was gone, and the rover kept moving.

"Dammit," said Mia as she picked herself up from the ground. "It didn't work."

"Wait," said Gizmo. A few seconds later, the rover came to a shuddering halt as the rear wheels seized up.

Mia let out a long, slow breath. "I wonder how many are still inside?"

"I am reading two heat signatures."

Mia looked at the droid. "You can do that?"

"Infrared. Simple, really."

Mia hefted her weapon. "Okay, I presume if there are only two still in there, then it must be Baptiste and Orban."

"That would be the logical conclusion."

"So, any ideas on how we get in there?"

"There are two airlocks. One at the rear, and another on the far side. It should be simple enough to hack the door controls."

"Except they'll know we're coming. We would be sitting ducks, like shooting fish in a barrel."

"Why would someone want to shoot fish in a barrel?"

"I don't know, Gizmo. It's just a saying."

"It makes no sense to me."

Mia handed the droid a plasma pistol. "Don't worry about it. Here, I reckon you're gonna need this."

The droid took the weapon and examined it. "Excellent. Gizmo is back in business."

"Just be careful not to fry any of the equipment in there. Remember, our objective is to reverse the evacuation protocols, so the gear needs to still function."

"Understood. I suggest I go in first to clear a path."

"No, too risky. I don't want anything happening to you. You're the only one who knows how to use that control console. I'll go."

"But Mia..."

"No buts, Gizmo. This suit is going to run out of air in five minutes. I don't really have a choice. Also, it's tough as dinosaur hide—it should withstand a few hits."

"We could both enter at the same time. You take the rear airlock, I will take the side. That way we split their resources."

Mia looked over at Gizmo again. "Okay."

"I will need to hack the door controls first." Already, Gizmo was disassembling the rear airlock control.

"Can you still see where they are?"

"Both are at the front of the rover, lower deck, directly in front of the rear airlock," said Gizmo as the outer door slid open. It turned its head to Mia. "There you go. I will get to the other one now. Wait for my signal." It moved off down one side of the machine as Mia clambered inside the airlock.

"Don't take too long, Gizmo. I've only got three minutes of air left."

"Are you ready?"

"As I'll ever be."

"Okay, start the sequence."

Mia hit the button on the inside of the airlock. The outer door closed, and the pressure began to build. She stood with her back to the side wall, keeping as low a profile as possible, and readied her weapon by dialing down the power. This way she was less likely to damage any of the electronics inside.

The inner door slid opened, and a hail of plasma fire came whizzing in. Most of it missed Mia; it just dissipated harmlessly off the outer door. One shot did glance off her left thigh, but the rugged EVA suit took most of the sting out of it.

The firing paused, and she chanced a quick glance to get oriented. Baptiste had positioned himself behind a stack of equipment and had just been distracted by the side airlock door opening. Mia took her chance and fired.

She hit him directly in the chest. He screamed and clawed at his throat as he dropped to the ground.

Mia flipped her visor opened, took a deep breath, and slowly moved into the rover's interior. "Gizmo, where's Orban?"

"In the forward cabin." The droid pointed to a door below the cockpit companionway. "He has still not moved."

"I'll go check on him. You keep an eye on Baptiste...and find that encryption key." Mia unclipped her helmet and placed it on a shelf. She considered taking the bulky suit off, as it seriously restricted her movements in the close confines of the rover interior, but decided to check on Orban first.

The cabin was a private space, with two bunks against the outer shell of the rover. In the lower bunk, the Montecristo head of security lay flat on his back, eyes closed. Mia checked his pulse. He was still alive, breathing steadily. Around his upper body and neck he had the telltale scorch marks of a close-range plasma blast. She had no way to tell how long he had been out, or how soon he would come to. It could be any moment; his breathing and heartbeat were strong.

"Gizmo, I need something to tie this guy up," Mia called out through the cabin door. "I think he's going to come around pretty soon."

"We have a problem," came the reply.

Mia stood up and came back out of the cabin. "What problem?"

"You know that dish antenna I ripped off the roof?"

"Yeah."

"We need it to transmit the signal back to Syrtis."

"Well, that's just great. Why didn't you think of that before you started tearing the rover apart?"

"Eh...it seemed like a good idea at the time."

"Can you put it back?"

"Yes, I can. But it will take a bit of time."

"Well you better get to it. There are a lot of people's lives at stake here."

The droid was already entering the side airlock. "On it."

Mia sighed. *Goddammit*, she thought. *Just when everything was under control, now this.* She sighed again and decided she'd finally had enough of the bulky EVA suit. Time to get out of it.

She put her newly acquired high-tech plasma weapon down and spent the next few minutes extracting herself from the suit's restrictive confines. It felt good to be rid of it. And with renewed vigor, she went in search of something to use to tie up Orban and Baptiste.

She found plenty of wire attached to the equipment in the rover, but it was all in use, and she didn't want to rip anything out in case it was vital for comms, particularly after what Gizmo had just done.

This is ridiculous, she thought. *There has to be something I can use.*

She started up the companionway steps into the cockpit; maybe she'd find something up there. It didn't take her long. Stacked in one of the cockpit lockers was a neat assortment of ratchet straps. "Perfect," she said to herself as she grabbed a bunch.

She heard the side airlock door opening. "Gizmo, you fix that antenna?"

But the response that came back was the sound of a plasma weapon being fired—at full power.

Mia spun around, all senses on high alert. She reached for her pistol, only to remember that she had given it to Gizmo, and the other one she had left down in the main cabin beside the discarded EVA suit. "Shit."

Very slowly and carefully, she moved to the companionway steps and peered into the cabin. "Gizmo?"

No reply.

She started down the steps and saw a fully conscious Vance Baptiste holding her high-tech plasma weapon, which was still aimed at the side airlock door. She faltered on the step, and he swung the weapon around at her.

"Ahh...Agent Mia Sorelli." He jiggled the weapon. "Looking for this?"

"Where's Gizmo?"

Baptiste jerked his head at the airlock. "Your droid is no more."

Mia took a tentative step down so she could look into the airlock. The inner door was open, and inside she could see an immobile Gizmo, a dark-gray scorch mark radiating from a blackened crater in its breastplate. "Gizmo...no."

Baptiste pulled out a smaller plasma pistol and threw the high-tech weapon down. "No more left in that. I used all its power putting a hole in your droid." He advanced toward her. "And you. You're a total pain in the ass as well as a complete moron." With a free hand, he unzipped the front of his jacket and patted the thick layer of armor underneath. "The latest in plasma blast insulation. Did you seriously think I would enter into a goddamn war zone without some personal protection?"

Mia backed up the steps, and Baptiste cautiously followed. She moved all the way into the cockpit as he began to ascend the steps. "You're a persistent bitch, I'll give you that. But now it's time to die."

Mia flung the ratchet straps at him. It was a futile gesture, a last gasp. He fired, but his aim was off. Nonetheless, the shot grazed her left shoulder. Not enough to put her out, but enough for searing pain to radiate out from the contact point.

She yelled out in pain and grabbed her arm as the numbness started to spread along her neck and arm. "Screw you," was the best she could manage as she slumped to the floor.

Baptiste, seeing his prey down and in no condition to fight back, relaxed a little and came fully into the cockpit. He stood over her and took a moment to adjust the plasma weapon. "I think I'll dial this all the way up to *certain death*. Why waste time trying to kill you with multiple shots? While it would be much more entertaining, I'm a bit pressed for time."

He carefully aimed the weapon at her head. "Good-bye, Major Sorelli."

Mia held her breath, closed her eyes, and waited for the end to come.

She heard the shot, smelled the tang of ozone—but felt nothing. She opened one eye and looked at Baptiste. His face bore a look of surprise, then his eyes rolled back inside his head and he dropped to his knees.

Standing behind him, plasma pistol in hand, was Orban Dent, his eyes fixed on Baptiste. He ignored Mia as he advanced, kicking Baptiste over so he lay flat on his back, and shot him in the head. Baptiste's face briefly erupted in flames, and the stench was almost over-powering.

"Bastard," said Orban, more to himself than to Mia. It was only then that he looked at her. "It's okay, I'm done killing for today." He stashed the pistol in the waistband of his trousers.

Mia shifted her position and looked up at him. "You two have a lover's tiff?"

Orban laughed. "Ha, not quite. He's simply a homi-cidal maniac. He deserved to die."

"Like Agent Frazer? Did he deserve to die, too?"

"What?" Orban looked a little confused, then his face brightened. "Ah...you think I killed him?"

"You more or less admitted it, last time we met."

He shook his head. "No, I didn't kill him. I was just trying to scare you off the investigation, make you think twice about continuing."

"So, who killed him?"

Orban seemed distracted, like he had no interest in all these stupid questions. He glanced around the cockpit, then back at Mia. He looked at her for a moment, considering something. "Would it surprise you to know that no one killed him? If anything, he killed himself."

"Bullshit."

"I don't mean he committed suicide. It was more just...neglect." Orban rested his back against the side wall of the cockpit and rubbed his chest. "You see," he continued, "I knew him reasonably well, me being the head of security for Montecristo Industries, him being an agent for MLOD. But his problem was obsessiveness. He would get so wrapped up in all his conspiracy theories that he neglected every other part of his life. He had no relationships worth talking about, he was barely able to feed himself, and of course he never did any maintenance on his accommodation module. And, in the end, it killed him."

Mia stayed silent for a beat, not sure if Orban was spinning her a pack of lies.

"But this is wasting time." He waved a hand, spun around, and started down the companionway steps.

"What about all those people in Syrtis?" Mia shouted after him. "Do they deserve to die, too?"

"They don't," he shouted back. "That's why we have to stop it."

Mia dragged herself up from the floor. Her left side was numb, she couldn't move her arm, and her left leg had minimal mobility. Nevertheless, she utilized those parts of her that still functioned to shuffle her way down into the main cabin of the rover.

Orban looked up from a console and waved the encryption key at her. "Well, here goes. Let's hope that droid of yours fixed the antenna."

Mia moved over and glanced at the screen. It displayed a scrolling list of text that she had difficulty deciphering. But one thing she did understand was the word *deactivated* flashing up after every block of code.

Orban looked up at her and nodded. "Looks like it worked."

Mia slumped down again on the floor. "Thank god for that."

They sat in silence for a moment before Mia finally spoke. "What I don't understand is, if you hated Baptiste so much, why wait so long to get rid of him?"

Orban stood up and moved over to the rear airlock. "Well, I'm no saint. In fact, I'm a complete bastard, really. But killing hundreds of people out of pure spite? That's simply not right. I couldn't let that happen." He opened a door to a large locker containing a rack of sleek EVA suits.

"Actually, it was Agent Frazer who planted the seed in my mind. He was always going on about some wild conspiracy theory or another, but he was right about siphoning off the components, and how that was indirectly killing people. I would argue it with him for hours, but it got me thinking. And for the first time ever I began to have my doubts...you know, about what Montecristo were doing." By now he had put on one of the EVA suits and was lifting down a helmet from the rack. "It probably would have stayed there, you know...just doubts. I might not have done anything about it if not for Baptiste's insanity. I had to stop him." He clipped on the helmet.

"Anyway, it's time for me to go. They'll be out from Syrtis soon, so I think you'll be okay until they get here. As for me, well, there's a shuttle waiting for me, and I'm going to take it." He held up the encryption key for her to see. "Now that I've got the keys to the house, I think I might just steal Baptiste's orbital. I don't think he'll mind." He stepped into the rear airlock. "By the way, if you're ever looking for a change of scenery, they could use someone with your skills in private security. Good money, ten times what they pay you in the MLOD. Lots of work out in the asteroid belt and the new colonies. Things are growing fast out there."

Mia gave a faint smile. "Thanks, but I'm good."

"Well, if you ever change your mind, you know where to find me."

"And where do I find you?"

He gave her a wry smile. "You're a detective. I'm sure you can figure it out. Anyway, gotta go. Maybe I'll see you around sometime." He gave her a brief salute, flipped down his visor, and closed the door.

22

AFTERMATH

Bright sunlight filtered down through the museum's domed roof and onto the rows of artifacts from the colony's past. The place was busy with tourists taking in the history and the general ambiance. But for Mia, there was only one artifact she had come here to visit. As she approached, she could see a young couple standing in front of the exhibit, discussing it.

"It looks so old and battered."

"Sure does. It's hard to believe they had to rely on such ancient technology."

"I think it looks cute. And I'm sure if it was working it would have some wonderful stories to tell."

"I doubt it. It's just an old maintenance droid."

"It says here that it played a pivotal role in the survival of the colony."

"Well, I suppose that's what maintenance droids do.

Hey look, over there. It's one of the early landers. Come on, lets go check it out."

They moved off.

Mia walked up to the exhibit and stood looking at it for a moment. "Well Gizmo, I came to say goodbye. I'm leaving soon, and well, I couldn't go without one last farewell."

"Mia!"

She looked around to see Bret walking toward her, waving a friendly hand.

"I've been looking everywhere for you."

"Well, now you've found me."

"I'll be bringing you out to the spaceport. The rover is ready and waiting for you. I've been designated your official driver."

"Okay, thanks."

He looked over at the droid. "I see they cleaned it up, got rid of the blast marks. You know, I always wondered why you never insisted on getting it fixed and brought back online."

"I had considered it, but the fallout from the Monte-cristo incident just became too much. Everything became a council issue. Everything was focused on rebuilding, and lots of politics surrounding the fair redistribution of all the components they found out in the Leighton waystation."

"Yeah, I guess so. Your new friend Lloyd did very well out of the whole thing, what with getting all those new contracts."

"Well, he earned it, I suppose."

"Say, I heard the investigation into Chief Becker's role in the whole affair is due to conclude soon. Looks like he might escape sanction."

"So I heard. But he won't be part of the MLOD anymore."

"Still, I thought they would nail him good and proper."

"Ah...you know what these things are like, Bret. Once the storm started to clear, everyone's mood changed. I think people started to see it all as a bad dream, something they wanted to forget. I mean, look—all the tourists are back. It's like it never happened."

"Yeah." He looked at the droid again. "And Gizmo is back where it all started."

Mia looked back at Gizmo again for a moment. "I really did want to get it back online, but then I thought, what for? Would it just end up being some celebrity droid, a kind of court jester to wheel out every so often and do tricks for the audience?"

"True." Bret nodded.

"And when everybody got bored, as they do, what would happen to Gizmo then? So, in the end, I reluctantly agreed with the council. This is the best place for it. After all, it is a national treasure. And, well, technically I did break the law in reanimating it the first time."

They stood in silence for a beat before Bret spoke again.

"So, you're really going back to Earth?"

"Yeah. They've offered me a diplomatic number. I get to swan around and do pretty much do nothing."

"You think you'll ever come back?"

Mia just shrugged.

Bret checked the time. "We better go. Don't want to miss the takeoff, or you'll be stuck here for another month."

Mia glanced back at the droid one last time and gave it a salute. "So long, Gizmo. Who knows, maybe we'll have another adventure someday."

THE END

I HOPE you enjoyed reading this story as much as I enjoyed writing it for you. If you did, then please leave me a review. Just a simple 'liked it' would be great, it helps a lot.

ALSO BY GERALD M KILBY

You can also find the next book in the series, Plains of Utopia: Colony Six Mars, here.

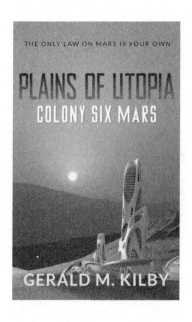

When an Earth-bound ship explodes on the launchpad in Jezero City, and the DNA from two bodies recovered at the site are found to be an exact match, Dr. Jann Malbec is convinced that they are the product of a covert cloning program.

ABOUT THE AUTHOR

Gerald M. Kilby grew up on a diet of Isaac Asimov, Arthur C. Clark, and Frank Herbert, which developed into a taste for Iain M. Banks and everything ever written by Neal Stephenson. Understandable then, that he should choose science fiction as his weapon of choice when entering the fray of storytelling.

REACTION is his first novel and is very much in the old-school techno-thriller style and you can get it free here. His latest books, **COLONY MARS** and **THE BELT,** are both best sellers, topping Amazon charts for Hard Science Fiction and Space Exploration.

He lives in the city of Dublin, Ireland, in the same neighborhood as Bram Stoker and can be sometimes seen tapping away on a laptop in the local cafe with his dog Loki.

Printed in Great Britain
by Amazon

41289087R00155